Alice

Patrick Bennett

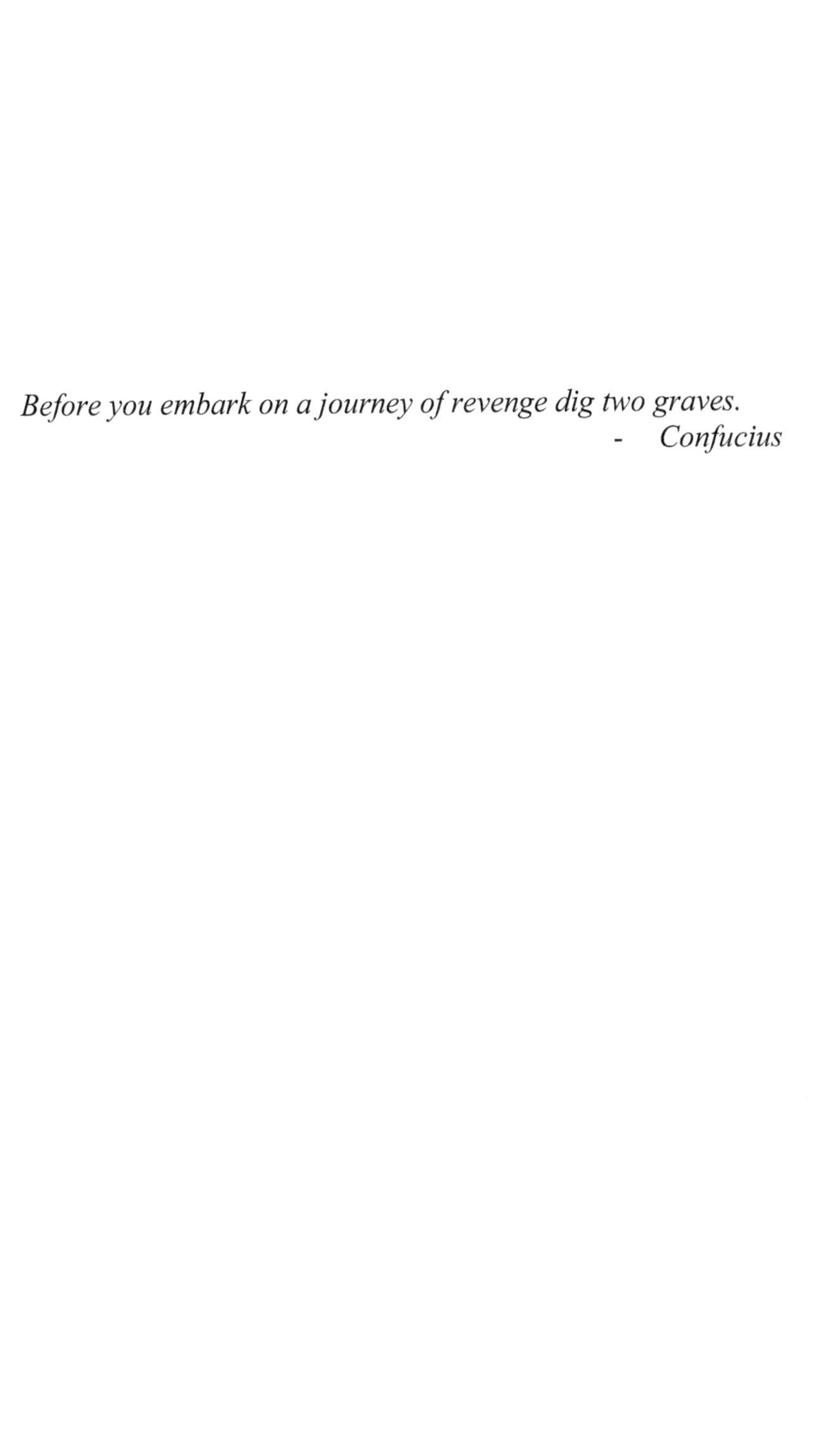

Before you embark on a journey of revenge dig two graves.

-   Confucius

1

The train rattles through Colchester and out into the more open countryside beyond. I like train journeys. I think most people do. A time to pause and reflect. And I do reflect, on the past fourteen years that have led me to this journey today. And I think about its purpose, a purpose that is not yet clear to me. In truth it is more an impulse; an impulse fourteen years in the making.

*

It was of course my own fault. At twenty-two no-one would get one over on me. I now cannot remember where the party was, whose party it was or how I came to be there. The people were mostly older than me, and richer, and better dressed. A few drinks in and I didn't feel too uncomfortable. I noticed a tall, dark girl looking over at me every now and then as she chatted without much interest to a short, bald man, who must have been twice her age. I noticed he kept touching her arm with his free hand and each time she moved it away. I decided she needed rescuing. A swig of wine and I'm on my way over.

'Hello there, what a surprise'.

She turned to me. 'Oh hello' and turned her back to the short man who took the hint. When he was out of earshot she asked 'Who are you?'

'I'm a professional rescuer of people from bores. I'm paid to go to parties like this to help people in distress.'

She paused for a moment as though she actually believed me and then laughed. 'He wasn't too bad. He's actually a friend of my father, trying to give me career advice'.
'Do you need it?'
'No, not really'.
'The inevitable question, so what do you do?'
'I'm secretary to the deputy manager of Hunterston and Griffiths'.
I should have walked away then. Why not just say – I'm a secretary. But I didn't. She was very attractive and the more I drank the more my centre of rationality descended towards my trousers. I braced myself for the return question. It came.
'So what do you do?'
'I'm a lorry driver'
'Really'
A single word conveying a wealth of meaning: *I'm wasting my time with this one. How weird, a lorry driver at a party like this. He doesn't look much like a lorry driver.* And I didn't. Long hair and hippy clothes. I wondered about telling her it was only a temporary thing until I went to college. I shouldn't need to but I did. Then the inevitable questions about what I was going to study and why, asked with little real interest. I wondered if I should cut my losses and clear off but she showed no signs of moving away. It's a great advantage being tall. Women are attracted to you for no good reason, tall women especially. People were starting to drift away.
'Where do you live?' I thought I might see her home.
'In North London but I'm staying here.'
I was by now quite drunk and she not much less. Somehow we ended up in a bed. She kept all her clothes on. After a brief drunken fumble we both fell asleep. I woke to find her standing by the bed.
'I've got to go to work'
'But it's Saturday'
'Makes no difference'
'When can I see you again?'

'Here's my number.'
'I hate arrangements like that. Can't you give me a day?' I must have still been drunk to wheedle in that way.
'Monday then but give me a ring first.'
I didn't ring her first. I hate phones. Although mum had one I hated to use it if anyone might hear me. For the first few years after it was put in I wouldn't go near it. Now it was Monday and I hadn't phoned her. I went to a call box at about six o'clock and phoned.
'But I told you to phone first. I'm doing something else now.'
Quit now Jim. She's a horror. But I didn't.
'Oh, really. That's a shame.' I let it hang.
'Well, look. I'm going to the pub with a couple of friends. You can come if you want'
'Okay, which pub?'
'The Cherry Tree, on Garforth Street in Islington. Do you know it? We'll be there about eight'.
'Right. I'll find it.'
Dave would have said – why are you always trying to prove you're an idiot. Yes it was all wrong but… Actually there was no but. I was just an idiot. It couldn't have been worse. Laura was there with two girlfriends.
'Laura says you're a lorry driver. That must be interesting'. This from Helen. A laugh from the other two.
'More interesting than you might imagine.'
'What twiddling your steering wheel and playing with your gearstick all the way up the motorway.'
Sarah's contribution met with even more laughter. They were becoming emboldened by drink and their collective spite. Another half hour of the same and I decided it was time to stop being an idiot and cut my losses.
'Nice to meet you all but I've got to go'.
Outside the pub I hit a fence, over and over again until my hand was bleeding. I was making so much noise that someone even came out of the pub to see what was happening. I cleared off.

I couldn't get it out of my mind. Why treat someone like that? What had I done to deserve it? What I had done was to be supine. They saw a victim and put the boot in. It was partly a class thing. The mercilessness of the middle class. A week went by and an idea began to grow. I phoned Laura.

'I didn't expect to hear from you again.'

'I know, sorry about walking out but it seemed to me that four was a crowd.'

'We went over the top a bit. Anyway what do you want?'

'I want to take you out to dinner.'

A pause. 'What, in a transport café?' Now I had the plan I could take the jibes. She was just making it worse for herself.

'Actually, have you heard of Monsieur Piriot's?' Of course she had. Everyone of her class and type had. It was one of the trendiest and most expensive places in North London.

'You want to take me there? It's ridiculously expensive.' But she hadn't said no. Something to boast to her friends about perhaps.

'I've had a bit of luck.'

'Oh really. What kind of luck?'

'I'll tell you about it when I see you.' We agreed a date.

'Where do you live? I'll pick you up.'

'It's ok. I'll meet you there.'

'Listen, I've got a car. I want to pick you up.' She took the bait.

I didn't have a car or suitable clothes. It was time to see Dave. I knew Dave from school. Unlike the dropout at 16 that I was, Dave had done his 'A' levels and gone on to university. He was in his first year with a brokering company and making a lot of money. None of that made any difference to our friendship, which was based mostly on a shared sense of humour. We could always make each other laugh.

'Dave I need to borrow your car.' The car being a blue MGB just six months old.

'Not lost your sense of humour then.'

'Seriously. I've got a hot date. I've promised to pick her up.'

'Why don't you take her in your lorry?

'Ha, ha. Listen mate, I'll make it up to you.'
'How's that then, seeing as you're a penniless wastrel?' You can tell he had a degree in English.
I knew he would lend it to me, mainly because he trusted my driving. We had once driven back from Scotland in a day. He was so hungover he was seeing double. I wasn't much better but I managed to do all the driving.
'If there's so much as a scratch on it…'
'Oh and I'll need to borrow that cream suit of yours'
'Jesus Christ. Anything else?'
'That'll do for now.'
'You cheeky toe rag. Fuck off before I change my mind.'
The car was an essential part of the plan. Without it, it wouldn't work. Even as I made the reservation I was having doubts. Supposing she followed me out. No surely not. In truth I was more worried about understanding the menu, not making a twat of myself.
Laura's house in Tenterden Road was an unremarkable, square-bay-fronted late Victorian semi, one in a whole street of them. If it was hers, she was doing well. She didn't let me in but came out as soon as I pulled up. Not much warmth there but her greeting was friendly enough. She had dressed in a low-cut green dress which really showed off her figure. Now what made me think this wasn't for my benefit!
'Nice house. Yours?'
'I share it with a friend'
'One of your nice friends of the other night?'
'No, not actually. You're not going to be funny, are you?'
'You were a bit cruel.'
'Shall we just forget that and enjoy our evening?' You can forget but I won't, I thought. And I don't think you're going to enjoy this evening as much as you think.
There was a car park at Monsieur Piriot's but I parked a little way away on the street.
'Why don't you park in the car park?'

'Too worried about being blocked in. I don't want to end up with any scratches, or worse. As you can guess, it's not my car.'
We went in. The décor might be described as restrained. Apart for some expensive looking paintings ranged along one wall there was little ostentation. The whole of one wall of the restaurant was of glass, looking out onto a courtyard appearing a little as though it might be part of a French country house. There were urns and planters with flowers cascading over their sides but again nothing too excessive. It was clear that Monsieur Piriot's saw itself as within the ambit of those of refined good taste. Every table had a candle burning and a small vase of some scented white flowers. The prices were as horrifically expensive as I had thought. I could see she was a little nervous about ordering the most expensive things but I encouraged her to have whatever she wanted. We had an aperitif and I ordered a bottle of wine, the cost of which represented my week's wages.
'So tell me about this bit of luck you've had.'
'My dad is friends with an on-course bookie who occasionally gets very good tips. Racing is not as straight as people think and some people make very good money by inside information. Anyway, this bookie told my dad of a dead cert that was likely to have an SP of 20 to 1.'
'I don't understand any of that. What's an SP?'
'Starting price. 20 to 1 means if you bet one pound and the horse wins you get twenty.'
'I had no money to bet with but my dad lent me some and happily the horse won, so here we are.'
'Why spend it on me?'
'We got off to a bad start and I wanted to put things right and see if we could move on.'
Her face didn't seem to agree with that idea however. Too bad. We meandered our way through the meal making desultory conversation. We started with lobster, which Laura had chosen. I had never eaten it before in my life and watched carefully to see how she tackled it. Thankfully it wasn't too complicated. For the main course we had Châteaubriand steak with a few skinny

vegetables. When I was growing up the proportions were exactly the other way round; masses of spuds and a sliver of meat. At least I knew where I was eating a steak; no need for written instructions. It was all very good and the wine was mellowing. She even managed to smile a few times and once laughed at a silly joke I told her. As we got nearer to the end of the meal I became more and more nervous. I kept looking at the door, which was a good twenty yards away. I ordered coffee. The moment had come.

'I've left my wallet in my jacket. Won't be a sec.'

I tried to walk slowly and casually to the door. I forced a smile at the maître'd who was hovering near the door and looking slightly puzzled. I knew it would be a mistake to offer him an explanation of where I was going. Monsieur Piriot's is not used to clients doing a runner. I continued my saunter to the car, resisting the urge to look back. I leaned into the car as though looking for something, then got in completely and in seconds I was away. I looked in the mirror. No-one had come out of the restaurant. That was part one of the plan successfully completed.

Two days later I braced myself for the phone call.

'Hello Laura.'

'You, you fucking bastard. Where's my money? I've reported you to the police.'

'What crime have I committed? Look I'm sorry about...'

'Never mind that. Where's my money?'

'Can you just listen for a minute? I've got your money. I want to explain what happened'

'I'm not interested. Can you imagine how I felt, left waiting there then having to pay myself?'

'I had forgotten my wallet. I couldn't face you. I know it was a terrible thing to do and all I can do is repay you the money. It's in cash. How can I get it to you? Can we meet at a tube station?'

'King's Cross would be best, tomorrow.'

'What time?'

'Seven.'

This is where it all went wrong. I had no intention of meeting her. For one thing I didn't have the money. And for another I wasn't finished with my little revenge plot. It was time for part two of the plan. The trouble was I didn't really know what part two was. I had the vague idea of going to her house but that's as far as it went. To do what? What would I do if her friend was in? If not, I reckoned I would have a clear hour. Twenty minutes to get to King's Cross, she would wait at least twenty minutes for me, and twenty to get back. I took the tube to Caledonian Road and walked the rest of the way to Tenterden Road. I walked past the house once. No lights on. I came back and knocked on the door, ready with an excuse. No answer. I thought about things for a minute as I stood in the porch. This was stupid. Her friend could come back any minute. I must have been on some sort of adrenaline rush. I didn't leave but went round to a side gate I had noticed. Locked. There was a large urn by the path. Standing on it I could reach over the gate and, just as I thought, there was a bolt which I could pull back. I heard a car come down the road and slow. Shit! It didn't stop. I was through the gate into the back garden. It was the sort of garden that is maintained by a contractor. Very neat and tidy, shrubs carefully planted but completely soulless. The fences either side were high. No chance of being seen by someone hanging out their washing, somewhat unlikely at seven o'clock anyway.

There were three steps up to the back door. The likelihood of it being open was not great but worth a try. Weird; not only was it not locked, it hadn't been closed properly. Very careless The back door led into the kitchen. Another door led into the hallway. My heart was thumping now. I stopped to think for a moment. If someone came in the front, my escape was out the back and through the side alleyway. I went back, opened the back door wide. Same with the door into the hall. There was only one door off the hallway. It was slightly ajar. A purplish light was showing in the room. I pushed the door a little and saw the source of the light, an aquarium, gently bubbling away. I pushed the door open a little more and there was Laura staring straight at me from an armchair. I let out a little yelp. In that endless moment, lasting only a few seconds, I went through every emotion. But the eyes were only staring, not seeing. I moved closer. She was slumped sideways in the armchair. Her arms hanging either side. She was wearing a dress, which had ridden up, and on her head what I thought was a Spanish mantilla. Only it wasn't. It was a veil of blood that had cascaded down her face and shoulder, black in the purplish light. By the chair was a decanter. I picked it up. It had blood and hair on it. Someone had given her a mighty whack or two.

What the bloody hell had happened here? Time to go. I retraced my steps, pulling the back door to and making my way up the side path. I used the urn again to put the bolt back. Someone was coming along the pavement. Nowhere to go. I ducked down and pretended to be doing something with the plants by the path, keeping my head well hidden. It was in any case getting quite dark now. Whoever it was didn't slow but just kept going. I left the garden and set off briskly to the tube station. My mind was racing. I took the tube to Finsbury Park and changed to the Victoria line. Then it struck me. I had left my fingerprints all over the house. Shit, shit, shit! But could they connect mc to Laura? She hadn't had a phone number or address for me. She didn't even know my surname. But what about the party? Could they trace who was there and who had invited who? I had to go back. I got off at Blackhorse Road. Surrendered my ticket and bought another. I hoped no-one was taking any particular notice. I decided to get off at Holloway Road and walk. I didn't want to be too identified with the nearest tube stop to Laura's house.

I turned into Tenterden Road and saw I was too late. There were several police cars and an ambulance. The friend must have come home. I walked back to Holloway Road and returned the way I had come. I tried to think things through. I came up with any number of ideas. None of them sensible. What would an innocent person do? I had arranged to meet her. She hadn't turned up. What would I do next? I would phone. That was the answer. When I got off the tube I went to a phone box. A man answered.

'Could I speak to Laura?'

'Who's that calling?'

'My name's Jim.'

'Jim what?'

'Sorry, who are you?'

'The police.'

'Oh. Has something happened?'

'Can you give me your name?' I did.

'And why are you phoning?'

'I arranged to meet Laura this evening and she didn't turn up. I wondered what had happened.'

'Laura Finnegan is deceased.'

'What. How. What's happened?'

'I can't tell you that. We'll need to speak to you. What's your address?' I told him.

It was a simple story that I would stick to. Keep as close to the truth as possible. I had forgotten my wallet on our evening out and arranged to meet Laura to repay the money. I didn't need to mention the fact that I'd fucked off and left her in the restaurant. They came to mum's house and seemed to accept my story. They asked me if I had ever been to the house. I told them that I had never been inside. Now I was in trouble if they took my fingerprints. I would never be able to convince them of the truth. They never did take my fingerprints. I heard later that the theory was that it was a burglary gone wrong. So they hauled in a load of burglars but no-one was ever charged. For months after, I jumped every time someone knocked at the door. But the more time passed the more it seemed I had got away it.

*

2

The train was coming into Ipswich, where I would have to change to a local train. I had an hour to wait so went off to find a pub. The place nearest the station was a bit shabby but I couldn't be bothered to walk further. After my long confinement you would think that I would have used any excuse to get out into the fresh air but actually things seemed to have worked out somewhat to the contrary. I had become habituated to having walls around me, or more specifically behind me. You learn to be wary. I wondered if Ipswich was where Dalby worked. There wouldn't be much in Saxmundham, which was little more than a village. In truth I knew nothing about him, except that he had married her. Did he even work? Was he super-rich and didn't need to work? Once I found the house I would know much more.

*

In September of 1973 my course started. There was a lot of work to be done, new people to meet, and I hardly ever thought about Laura. Just occasionally the sightless, staring eyes would come back to me in a quiet moment. In the second term I had a placement in North London which meant taking the Piccadilly line out to Turnpike lane. It was inevitable that I would recall that panicky journey of a year ago. I should never have gone near that house again but I was intrigued by the murder. One evening on my way back home I got off at Caledonian Road and walked to Tenterden Road. I had no clear plan. I might just take a look at the house. There was a light on in the living room. I walked up the path and rang the bell, prepared to make some excuse and bugger off as quickly as possible. My mouth felt dry and when a young woman opened the door I stumbled over my words.

'I was just…I wondered…I was a friend. Sorry, my name's Jim, I was a friend of Laura.' I suddenly realised that this person might have no idea who Laura was.

'Laura used to live here'

'I know, I was her housemate'

'Sorry, Laura never told me your name.'

'It's Alice.'

'Well the thing is Alice, I was just wondering if the police had ever come up with anything.'

'Do you want to come in for a minute?' I wasn't expecting that. By now I was desperate for a drink.

'Actually, do you fancy going for a drink? I've had a long day and I could do with one.'

She did and we went to the local. It seemed that the police hadn't come up with anything more than their original burglar theory. We chatted about the usual things that people do when they're getting to know each other. It was interesting that she asked me very little about how, and how well I had known Laura, which I found odd. Anyway, we seemed to get on well and I took the chance and asked if I could see her again. She seemed taken aback. Maybe she had somebody else but she gave me her phone number. I knew it already of course.

I waited a week or so and then phoned. We agreed to meet in the same pub. Alice was very easy to be with. We had a similar sense of humour, enjoyed the same kind of music and over a period of a few weeks saw more and more of each other. It seemed inevitable that we would become lovers and not long after that I moved into number 33. After the first flush of heady passion, lasting a year or so, like many couples, we settled into a comfortable routine. My course had gone well and I was starting to look for a job. Alice was a civil servant on a reasonable income and it was she who paid most of the household expenses, with no complaint about my meagre contribution. It was interesting that Laura was scarcely ever mentioned, though I did once ask Alice how she was able to afford the mortgage. She told me that there was no mortgage. They had had an insurance policy which meant that if one of them should die the mortgage would be paid off.

In July 1975 I started my new job, which gave an uplift to our income and we started to think about a move. Tenterden Road was starting to change. A couple of wine bars had opened further along the street and there was often noise late at night. We started to look for something further out. We finally found a house we liked in Southgate. The long weary journey of buying another house, selling ours, and the inevitable 'chain' was finally approaching its end in March of 1976. One day, packing stuff in boxes I asked Alice:
'I've sometimes wondered how you were able to stay in this house after what happened.'
'I suppose it seemed too much trouble to move.'
'Yes, but didn't you feel afraid, worried that whoever did it might come back?'
She was silent for a long time, then: 'It never occurred to me.'
I thought to myself, it certainly would have occurred to me. I had the feeling that she wanted to drop the subject, so I left it.
The following morning, it was a Sunday, we were lying in bed entwined in post-coital drowsiness when it seems I decided to prove to the world that I really was a complete idiot.
'Do you want to know a secret?'
'Don't tell me, you're secretly a transvestite.'
I laughed. 'No it's something to do with this house. Something I'm happy to be leaving behind.'
She turned to face me. 'What?'
An ominous feeling took hold of me. 'It doesn't matter. It's nothing important.'
'Yes it is. Tell me.'

'Well you've got to keep this secret.'
'Alright.'
'I had been in this house before I met you.'
'What, when you were going out with Laura?'
'No, not then.' So I told her the story of my visit to the house and finding Laura dead. I knew even before I started that it was a massive mistake.
'So it was you.'
'No I didn't kill her.'
'No, the fingerprints. The police found several sets of prints they couldn't match to anyone. They were yours.'
'Must have been'
Things were very quiet for the rest of the day but we went to work as usual on the Monday with nothing further said. I was surprised to find Alice not at home when I got back. She was always back before me. She came back half an hour later and mumbled something about some work she had to finish. The coldness hadn't diminished and I realised that it was going to be a long haul if ever we were to get back to our former closeness. We were woken at six the next morning by a clatter at the front door. I went down.
'What on earth…'
'James Mallinson?'
'Yes, what's up?' But I knew.
'I'm Detective Inspector Collinson and this is Detective Constable Dewar. I'm arresting you on suspicion of the murder of Laura Finnegan.' They gave me the usual warning and took me upstairs to get some clothes. Alice had left the bedroom and shut herself in the bathroom. I expected to be handcuffed but wasn't. They seemed to sense that I wasn't going to run away or be violent. They put me in the back seat of the car with the constable.
'I didn't do it.' This to the man beside me. The inspector turned round.
'You'll get plenty of chance to tell your story.'

At Holloway police station I went through some kind of checking-in procedure which I hardly noticed. I was turning over in my mind what must have happened. Alice must have gone to the police after work. Did she really think that I had done it, or was she disgusted about my 'burglary'? I couldn't have blamed her for the latter but, as I was to discover much later, my ideas about her motivation were way off the mark.

My first time in a police cell. It was a grubby, cream-painted room about eight by six, a none too clean toilet in the corner and a bench with a blanket. After about half an hour a uniformed constable looked in and brought me some toast and a cup of tea. I wanted to get on with the interview, to tell my side of things but I realised that keeping you waiting was part of the tactic, hoping you would 'cough.' The two-hour wait gave me plenty of time to reflect on my stupidity, my big mouth, the eternal show-off. The awful thing was that I was starting to feel guilty, to feel that I had done something terrible. Yes, I had in a sense broken into a house, though in fact I hadn't broken anything but I hadn't harmed anyone. No-one knew I had been in the house until I told Alice. And that was the thought that kept coming back to me – 'until I told Alice.' You could say that it was a case of self-harming.

After about two hours I was taken to the interview room. I was surprised to see that the Inspector was not there. There was the constable I had seen earlier and another middle-aged man who introduced himself as Sergeant Miller. He asked me if I wanted a solicitor to be present. I didn't. I just wanted to tell my story.

'So James, or is it Jim, or Jimmy?'

'Jim.'

'OK Jim, I need to remind you that you are still under caution. Tell us what happened at 33 Tenterden Rd on 10th of April 1973.' This was Miller speaking. The constable had a notepad and I guess his job was just to take notes.

I had decided by this time that I needed to slightly embellish the story. The truth made me sound like a psychopath. Just what I didn't need.

'I need to go back a bit. I took Laura to a restaurant about a week before the date in question. I forgot my wallet and Laura had to pay. She was furious, as you can imagine, but I promised to repay her. We arranged to meet at Kings Cross so I could hand over the money. Don't ask me why but I decided to play a trick on her. I thought I would go to the house first and see if I could get in. If I could, I would leave the money there and then go to Kings cross and tell her I'd lost the money on the way there. She would then find it when she got home.'

The further I got into this story the more implausible it sounded. By the time I had finished I was starting to think that I would have been better off telling the truth, even though it reflected so badly on me. The officers made no comment.

'Tell us exactly what happened when you got to the house.' I did so.

'So you found the body in the armchair, then what?'

'I realised I needed to get out of there as quickly as possible, so I left the way I came.'

'You say the back door was ajar when you arrived.' I confirmed that it was.

'But Miss Travis tells us that it was locked when she left in the morning and the same when she got home and found the body. How do you account for that?'

'I can't. How could I have got in otherwise?' Miller didn't answer that. It seemed to me that it was not a very important point and I couldn't understand why he was going on about it. I had admitted going into the house, after all.

'Okay so you were standing in the living room with the body. Did you do anything, touch anything?'

'No. I told you. I got out as quickly as possible.'

'In that case why were your fingerprints on the decanter that killed Miss Finnegan?

Shit! I'd forgotten about that.

'Well I thought I heard something upstairs. I thought there might be a burglar up there. I picked it up to defend myself.' Even as I said it I knew it sounded ridiculous. What's that expression, when you are in a hole…

'You didn't think you were interfering with an important piece of evidence?'

'No, I wasn't thinking at all. I was in a panic.'

'I don't know how much you know about the law. At the moment you think you're going to get away with this. Well you're not and you should know that an early confession and guilty plea saves the criminal justice system a lot of trouble and because of that you could get a discounted sentence. You might want to think about that. We'll take a break now.'

Sitting in that awful cell I came to realise how easy it must be to confess, even to confess to something you haven't done. The grinding monotony wears you down. You just want something different to happen, to get things over with. Of course you don't get things over with. It's just the start of a new monotony in a different place. They gave me some lunch, then it was back to the interview room.

The sergeant had been replaced by the inspector. I wondered why. New tactic? New information?

'Tell us about the evening you spent with Laura and her friends.'

How did they know about this? It can only have come from Alice. Laura must have told her.

'What about it?'

'You left early. Why was that?'

'Bit bored I guess.'

'Bored or humiliated? Wasn't it the case that they were taking the rise out of you? I expect you felt very angry about that, wanted to get your own back in some way. Isn't that it?'

'No not at all.'

'So you went to see Laura. You had an argument and you lost your temper, hit her with the decanter, probably didn't mean to kill her. Understandable enough. Am I right?'

'No, I told you, she was already dead.'

'Listen to me. I've been in the police force a long time. I know how things work. You cough for this, saying you didn't mean to

kill her, you just lost your temper, and you may, I say may, get manslaughter. You could be out in four or five years.'
'What's the use? I didn't do it.'
I was taken back to the cell but only for half an hour before I was brought out and formally charged. All the familiar clichés ran through my head – this isn't really happening, I'll wake up in a minute. But it was happening and became ever more real when I used my one phone call to phone mum, the last person I wanted to speak to. Neither she nor dad were in the best of health and needed no extra burden added to their day.
'I'm in a bit of trouble. I'm at the police station. They're keeping me in.'
'What sort of trouble? What have you done?'
'I haven't done anything. It'll all be sorted out but could you ask Steve to bring some stuff to Holloway police station.' Asking my brother to do anything that wasn't to his own advantage was like asking to him to empty his bank account in your favour. Five years older than me, he always looked down on me as a spoilt brat of a ne'er-do-well. An opinion I was about to confirm.
'What sort of stuff?'
'A change of clothes, some underwear, a washbag'
'But all your stuff's at Alice's.'
'I don't want him to go there. I've still got some clothes at home and he'll have to buy the stuff for the washbag. That'll break his heart.'
'What?'
'Nothing, would you just ask him to do that?'
She would and it was starting to dawn on me how all this was rippling out to involve others. What about my job. I'd have to get Steve to phone them. He got there surprisingly quickly. Must have made some excuse to get away from his desk. They brought me out to see him. He looked concerned. Not what I'd expected at all. I thought he would have that rather sneering, just what I would expect of you look.
'I've got your stuff. What on earth have you been up to?'
'I've been charged with Laura's murder.'

'Who's Laura?' I explained.
'But you didn't do it, surely?'
'Of course not. It's a complete cock-up. Thanks for bringing the stuff. Could you do one more thing for me? Could you phone work and tell them what's happened?'
'Of course, anything else I can do?' I was seeing a new Steve. Perhaps brotherly love did exist after all.
'No. Thanks again.' He left looking more worried than ever.

After a more or less sleepless night I was taken off to the magistrates' court at Highbury Corner. I was given a solicitor who did little more than tell me what the procedure would be. It was inevitable that I would be remanded. He was not interested in my case. It was all over in a few minutes. From the court I was taken to Pentonville. I think I was more curious than apprehensive. What was prison really like? After the admission procedure I was taken up to my wing. I was to be put in a cell with another remand prisoner, Arnold, a 56-year old, accused of defrauding the company he worked for, I was told by the warder. 'You'll be alright with him. Quite harmless.' The warder, an older man, seemed to be taking some trouble to reassure me. I wondered why. After all I was a murderer as far as he knew. Arnold sat on his bunk. There was one each side of the cell, by the side of which was a small cupboard. There were blankets on the bed and under Arnold's bunk a plastic chamber pot. I reached out my hand to Arnold.
'Jim.' He looked surprised but then slowly put out his hand.
'Arnold.'
'What happens now?'
'In a few minutes we'll be let out for association and then it will be lunch time.'
'What's association?'
'You can mingle with the other prisoners on the wing, play games, watch the TV if anything's on.'
As he spoke the door was unlocked and pulled open.

'Come with me. I'll show you what to do.' We clattered down the stairs to the association area. The other prisoners drifted down. Some started playing cards, or dominoes or just chatted. After a while one of them came up to me.

'Hello new boy. What you in for then?' I knew I had to be careful from now on. I knew there was a pecking order in prisons, which most likely was established very early on. I looked straight back at my inquisitor and said the one word.

'Murder.' Nothing else. I continued to stare at him.

'Not very talkative then.'

'No, not very.' I turned my back on him, expecting to be thumped but nothing happened. I became aware of food smells emanating from the kitchens, which were where I knew not. These smells mingled with the dominating prison smell, which was a mixture of sweat, piss, shit and tobacco smoke. The smoke smell was the least objectionable. I was to learn later that almost everyone smoked. It seemed to me that at least part of the reason was to mask all the other somewhat more unpleasant smells.

3

My hearing didn't come up until six months had passed. Before that my cellmate went for his trial. His story, which I slowly came to know, was a sad one. He was married to a younger woman who had taken to living beyond their means. She didn't work but spent a great deal of time and money shopping, and in order to pay for her shopping habits Arnold had started embezzling his company's funds. He was an accountant and had been with the company since he was a young man. His crime was seen as being all the worse for the fact that he was a trusted senior employee and a personal friend of the chairman of the company. Arnold's wife's visits were infrequent; something about which he was rather glad as she spent their time together complaining about how difficult it was to live on benefits. I was shocked when Arnold told me how little this in fact was. I had not thought about this before, the devastating effect on the family of a prisoner. Happily his two daughters were grown up and still living at home, and thus could contribute to the household finances. He wasn't at all looking forward to being back with his wife and just before he was taken away to go to court he said with a wink, 'I hope they don't let me out too soon.' I heard later that he got two years.

I had the cell to myself for a couple of weeks before Dennis moved in. Dennis was a forger, not of banknotes but of paintings. He was a very clever artist and could imitate the styles of a number of modern painters. His collaborator was a London gallery owner who sold Dennis's paintings on a no questions asked basis, implying that they were genuine works but that their provenance was a little dubious. They were eventually rumbled by a buyer who had bought a number of paintings, which he showed to an expert in modern art. Dennis had a completely insouciant attitude to his imprisonment. He didn't expect to get a long sentence and felt that it was a price he was prepared to pay. He had made a great deal of money from his work which he told me was very well hidden.

Finally the day came. I felt that we were as well prepared as we could be. Both Dave and Steve were there for the first day, and Steve intermittently thereafter but Dave could only manage that first day. Steve had persuaded mum and dad not to come, of which I suspect they were rather glad. From the outset I had the feeling that things were not going well. The judge was a miserable old sod who had clearly made up his mind. He had a very antagonistic attitude towards my barrister, who I have to say was very good indeed. There were two main points telling against me. The first was the fingerprint evidence, which of itself made a much stronger case than could my rather thin story of how the prints actually got there. The second was Alice's evidence. I have to say she looked wonderful. She wore a smart grey suit and her hair was tied back into a bun. The overall impression she gave was one of modesty and seriousness. She described firstly the scene at the pub which Laura had recounted to her. She then went on to tell how we had met and established a relationship. Then came the perjury. According to her, I had confessed to having a violent row with Laura and hitting her with the decanter. It was after that that she had gone to the police.
My barrister's attempts to break down this lie, to damage her credibility came to nothing. She gave a very good performance and stuck to her story. After all the evidence had been heard, my legal team felt themselves to be in a quandary. None of the

evidence contradicted the possibility of a plea of manslaughter. Clearly the murder was not premeditated and everything pointed to a sudden impulsive act on my part. Discussions were held with the prosecution and the message came back that yes, they would accept a plea of manslaughter. Both my barrister and solicitor urged this course of action on me. They thought I might end up serving only four of five years. I couldn't do it. I couldn't plead guilty to a crime I hadn't committed. I would put my trust in the jury. The judge's summing up was not helpful. It was subtle but it was clear where he was leading the jury. I had been told that there were two bad indications in jury behaviour. The first was a quick decision, and the second if they refused to look at the defendant when returning to court. My jury scored two out of two so the verdict came as no surprise.

My new cell was in D wing, the home of long term prisoners. I was put in a cell with Jock, who did not look best pleased to see me. He was a short, thick-set man with a permanent, exophthalmic stare. I guess he was in his mid-thirties. Before I was barely through the door he laid down the rules for our cohabitation. I said nothing, not least because his Glaswegian accent was almost impossible to understand. He asked me what I was in for. I asked him to give me some headspace before we started exchanging biographies. He didn't look happy with that but at last shut up. The coolness between us lasted a week or so before I felt able to make an attempt at better relations. Once the ice was broken it was apparent to me that Jock, despite his slightly menacing demeanour, was quite a reasonable bloke. He was an armed robber, serving seven years for his latest blag. He had gone into a building society and got trapped by their security doors.

I asked him why he seemed so miffed when I turned up. It seems he had had the cell to himself for several weeks and was rather hoping it would stay that way. He told me about his previous cellmate:

'No more than a boy. Shouldnae been in here. Dad bought him a sports car for his twenty-first. Went off with a load of his mates, got pissed up and killed a little girl. She and her mum were on a zebra crossing. The mum's crippled, in a wheelchair. Causing death by dangerous driving. Couldnae hack it. Crying his eyes out. Kept saying my dad was supposed to fix it. What he meant was his dad was gonna give the family a whole pile of money and he would get a lighter sentence. Dunno what happened. Anyway, he got a five stretch. We were down in association. You know the blokes don't go to the bog until the last minute before bang up so they don't go so much during the night. So no-one's in the bogs for a couple of hours before bang up. When we went in you could see the blood, a great sheet of it all across the floor. Did a proper job. Slashed along the veins, not across. He meant it. He was a spoilt little rich boy but I couldnae help feeling sorry for him.'

'God, that's an awful story.'

'You're not much older.'

'Don't worry, I won't be going down that road.'

And so we settled into peaceful coexistence. It was important to get on with your cellmate, if no-one else. Any difficulties that came along he would stand by you. There is a pecking order in prison and a lot of bullying. It's important to stand up to it from the outset. This hierarchy mainly concerns the hard men, professional criminals for whom so-called 'respect' is important. What I quickly realised is that it's possible to stand outside this structure by making yourself seem middle class or academic or slightly potty. Although I wasn't middle class, I could put up a good act of being so. I tended not to join in with the games and the television viewing but rather stayed in my cell or sat apart reading. I spent a lot of time in the library. As a child I had loved going to the library. We used to walk a couple of miles to Leytonstone library every two weeks or so, our four books tucked under our arms. For me the library was like an Aladdin's cave and it remained so as an adult. My interest in the library was noted and after a year or so I was given a job there. Working in the library was considered to be a cushy number and there was some disgruntlement from one or two others who thought they should have been given a job there. The truth was that these characters were more interested in the cushiness than the books. There were two other librarians, Ray and Edward. Things were a little cool at first but I insisted on being cheerful and friendly and they soon warmed up. Over time I got to know their stories. Ray was serving five years for fraud. He had had a racket setting up 'long firms'. He explained to me how it worked. He would set up a company and buy and sell goods in the normal way. Once he had established himself as a trustworthy businessman with his suppliers he was able to buy goods on extended credit, which was usually three months. He would then buy a whole lot of stuff from different suppliers, sell it off cheaply, then disappear before the bills arrived. He would repeat the whole process with an entirely new company. He did this for several years before being finally rumbled. Ray was quite philosophical. He had a pile of money hidden away for when he got out. In those days there was no mechanism for recovering the proceeds of crime.

Edwards's story was truly tragic. He had been a solicitor. He was in his late fifties, having served ten years of a life sentence. He had lived in a rather fine house in Hampstead. Coming home one day he caught a burglar rifling through his wife's jewellery. Edward had been middleweight boxing champion in the army back in the thirties and he was still pretty handy when he encountered the burglar. He decided to teach him a lesson and set about him. He beat him unconscious and then threw him out on the street. The young man wasn't discovered for some hours and by then he was dead of a brain haemorrhage. There was considerable debate about whether Edward should be charged with murder or manslaughter. What tipped it in favour of the former was the conclusion that had an ambulance been called promptly the burglar might have been saved. The fact that Edward didn't call an ambulance suggested that he was content for him to die.

After about a year in Pentonville my appeal came up. It is usual for defendants who have received a life sentence to be granted an appeal. I had a new brief this time who seemed little interested in my case. I wondered how much time he had spent studying it. We were appealing against conviction on two grounds. The first that the judge's summing up had not been balanced and the second that the case rested almost entirely on the fingerprint evidence. The appeal judges were not convinced and confirmed the original verdict. I was surprised how little disappointed I was. My brief seemed only to be going through the motions and his lack of enthusiasm had me giving up hope long before I knew the actual verdict.

*

4

On the little train that was taking me to Saxmundham. I wondered what she looked like now. She would be in her late thirties. Had she grown fat and slutty? I very much doubted it. She was someone who liked to be in control, if only of herself. What about Dalby? Might he even be sitting on this train? Was that him over there? I started to imagine him. A decent, law-abiding middle class chap, devoted to his wife and children, or was he a wife beater and child abuser. I knew that the latter was impossible unless she had had a complete change of personality. I started to have more doubts about this journey. So often the thought crosses the mind; how did I come to be at this place at this moment in time?

*

At first I had visitors. Being in a London prison meant it wasn't too difficult for mum and dad to get to see me. I'm not sure they really believed I was innocent. Like a lot of respectable working class people they had great faith in the police and the judicial system. Could such a terrible mistake have been made that their own son would be convicted of a murder he hadn't committed? I could see that they found it difficult to doubt a system that they had put such faith in all their lives. On their visits there were long pauses. Not surprising really. We talked very little at home and they never really had much to say to each other either. Mum stopped coming after the first year and in fact I never saw her again. She died of cancer in February of 1978. I think dad blamed me for the way she went down so quickly after the cancer had been diagnosed, although he never said so of course. He struggled on for the first three years, his visits becoming less and less frequent before stopping altogether. He died two years after mum. As a 'model prisoner' I was allowed to go to his funeral. I was kept apart from the other people at the crematorium. They looked over at me and Auntie Jane gave me a big smile but the rest were unreadable. Steve was allowed to come across to sit with me. We said nothing, there being nothing to say.

Steve had kept up the big brother concern for me that he had shown when I was first arrested. He came to see me every month for the first couple of years and then less frequently, finally stopping after five years. I didn't blame him. His wife never liked me and I guess she resented the time his visits took him away from the family. In truth we had very little to say to each other. He would tell me about his work and what the kids had been up to. They had been toddlers when I went inside so I didn't really know them and their activities and achievements meant little to me. Dave had been as good a friend as ever. His visits were not regular. He would just turn up when the fancy took him. At first we would make each other laugh, as always, despite the situation. As time went by things became more strained. Dave had always believed in my innocence and it bothered him to see me banged up. He became even more upset after my appeal failed. On his last visit he was in tears as he was leaving and I told him not to come again. He just nodded and left.

So after five years I had no more visitors but it didn't matter. Prison life very quickly becomes your norm, almost as though you never had another life. The outside world is the one that is unreal. In 1983 I was moved to Lewes. This was a modernised prison with better facilities. The move was partly a reward for being no trouble to anyone. I was determined to serve the least possible time. My tariff had been set at fourteen years but that didn't mean I would necessarily get out in that time. First of all I had to acknowledge my guilt. I took a completely pragmatic attitude to this. If that's what was needed then I would comply. Secondly I had to convince the authorities that I was a reformed character and no threat to anyone. This I tried to do by never causing trouble, never complaining, following all the courses, group discussions, whatever. I knew that it was all about box ticking. I wanted to make it easy for them to tick all the right boxes.

*

At the station only one other person got off the train. Not far from the station was the Bell Inn. This would do me perfectly. I was in no hurry. I needed time to plan. Pubs had changed; gone were Formica-topped tables and bright lights. Now it was wall lights and oak veneer. People had changed too. Nobody dressed smartly to go for a drink. Jeans seemed to be the order of the day for both sexes. Hair was shorter too. Prices had changed. It was difficult to adjust to producing notes for a pint of beer rather than loose change. Inside we had heard vaguely about the hyperinflation of the Thatcher years but it meant nothing to us, where all our needs were provided for.

I had checked in for an indefinite stay. The woman at reception seemed unconcerned. I doubted they had many people staying. My room was a good size and clean. I was still getting used to the feeling of being able to walk in and out of a room when I felt like it; to have my own shower. I lay on the bed and thought what it meant for someone like me to be free. To be able to go where I liked and do what I pleased. How much we take that for granted. No-one who hasn't been imprisoned truly understands freedom. And so was I going to chuck this all away? Create some kind of scene with her and be put back inside? A life sentence is just that. You never finish serving your sentence, inside or out. You can be recalled at any time for any reason. The closer it came to …to what? I didn't know and because I didn't know I

29

started to worry. Was I going to repeat history? Do something impulsively stupid, again?

I needed a drink and something to eat. Food had changed too. No more gammon and pineapple and duck à l'orange. Half the things on the menu were unknown to me. I played safe and ordered a steak. The steak downed with several glasses of wine I felt mellow, and more confused than ever about the purpose of my journey. I thought I would take a look at Saxon Road, get my bearings for when…but when was when? My thinking had got no further than the burning desire to find her. Now that I was minutes away from her, all the urgency had drained from me. It took less than ten minutes to reach Saxon Road. It was a street of large detached houses, by the look of them a 1970s development. I walked a little way along the road in order to see the numbers of the first few houses – evens. So No.17 was on the other side. I walked back to the corner. By counting along I could see which was hers. There was a small blue car in the drive and lights in the upstairs windows. Putting the children to bed maybe. Did they even have children? On the corner where I was standing there was a building which announced itself as a community library. It had clearly been something else before, maybe a bank or a building society. There were tables and chairs close by the window. It would make a good observation post. It opened at 08.30. Perfect. I would return tomorrow.

*

There was very little trouble on the long term wing. There was an understanding between prisoners and warders that we could either make life difficult for each other or the opposite. Since we were all in for the long haul it made sense to get on with our jailers. As a result there were little privileges made available to us that were not given to short-term prisoners. Trouble in prison is almost always caused by prisoners with short sentences; the miserable little scroats who would break into your house, make a mess of the place, steal a television which they would sell for next to nothing and be no better off. They were the type who would be endlessly in and out of prison causing trouble everywhere they went. We were thankful not to be in with them. There was no question of the moral superiority of warders over prisoners or of prisoners over other prisoners. We were all in there to do our time and that's all that mattered. Two on our wing in Lewes were whole-lifers. One had murdered his whole family - his wife, two boys and a girl – in a fit of jealous rage over his wife's affair; an affair it turned out she hadn't been having. The other was a serial killer. He had taken to strangling prostitutes. He was credited with four deaths but was suspected of more. We hardly ever saw either of them since they rarely emerged from their cells. For the rest, there were several murderers like me and the remainder were serious 'career' criminals, armed robbers and the like.

Sex was dealt with mainly by masturbation, an urge which it was generally agreed declined over the years. There were a few prisoners who formed 'close' friendships and these men at their own request were moved to a wing with others of a like persuasion. One of our warders who had previously worked on that wing expressed vehemently his disgust of what went on. 'You wouldn't believe it' was his stock phrase.

At Lewes I became something of a governor's pet. In both Pentonville and here I had taken a lot of interest in the library. At Pentonville I helped reorganise the collection so that it made more sense to prisoners who were less than wholly literate. Only a minority of prisoners made use of the library at either prison. This was because they were either functionally illiterate or just uninterested, books never having been part of their life. At Lewes there had been literacy classes given by an outside tutor but this had been stopped after funding had been cut. I thought I might be able to do something and so asked to see the governor. I was taken to her office. It was an austere space without any softening touches at all, no family photos, colourful fabrics, or knick-knacks on her desk. Nothing to suggest this woman had a life outside the prison. There was a desk, several chairs, a filing cabinet and in one corner a few cups and a kettle. Her expression was as severe as her office and I started to think that my idea was ridiculous and would be treated as such. The prison officer accompanying me looked as nervous as I felt. Then to my surprise, just when I was on the point of wishing I could back out of the room, she gave me a beaming smile and said 'I hear you want to start literacy classes for some of your fellow prisoners'.

'Y-yes, I thought, I wondered…' I was so taken aback I couldn't put together a sensible sentence.

'Why don't you sit down and explain your idea?'

'I thought I might start a small group for some of the prisoners on my wing.'

'Have you got any experience?'

'Not with literacy work but I have worked with small groups.' The honest truth was I had worked with one group, and that not for very long. I thought to myself that she wouldn't be asking these kinds of questions if she was going to dismiss my idea out of hand and indeed she didn't. Things got even better when she asked me what resources I would need and promised to supply them.

On the way back to my landing I talked to Taff Jones, the warder who had accompanied me. 'Did she scare you as much as she scared me, Taff?'

'You're not kidding Jim, she's a tough cookie but always fair, I've found.'

'So it looks like we're up and running.'

'Who did you have in mind?'

'I don't know. They'll have to self-select.'

'I'm not sure you'll get anybody. Bit humiliating being taught by a fellow prisoner.'

'We'll have to see. Will you put the word around?'

There were four takers. We were given a little room, a whiteboard, paper and pens. Everyone was very tense. The difficulty for these blokes was that they saw themselves as hard men but illiteracy was a weakness. I thought that everything depended on this first session. Humour had to be the key.

'Are you lot as nervous as I am?' Was my opening shot. Someone chuckled.

'I know this can be a sensitive subject so I want us to be able to trust each other and feel that we're in this altogether. So can I ask that we all shake hands with each other.'

To my amazement they didn't tell me to fuck off but actually did as I had asked. We started with some very simple reading tasks. I needed to find out their level. It was soon apparent that they were all semi-literate. They could slowly get through simple words but found less familiar words and complex sentences difficult. I encouraged them to help each other when they got stuck and this they did. So we got through that first hour, an hour that seemed like ten.

I was gratified when all four turned up for the next session. I had no real idea what I should be doing so I tried out different ideas to see what worked out best. I produced a pornographic gapfill text which caught their interest. Mac said 'You dirty bastard,' and they all laughed. As the weeks went by we settled into a routine and I could see that they looked forward to this diversion from the normal prison routine. Progress was slow but nevertheless measurable. There was a lot of humour and mickey-taking, which actually made the whole thing work. About week six or seven I was doing a gapfill with them where Chas was struggling to work out the missing word. Eventually he just said 'twat!' And we all laughed. We moved onto Terry who said, 'I know all the missing words.'

'Go on then.'

'Twat, twat, twat, twat, twat, twat.'

Of course they all fell about laughing, which got even worse when I said in a schoolmasterly fashion:

'Actually that is not the correct answer.'

We were making so much noise that one of the prison officers came in to see what was happening.

'Everything alright?'

'It's alright Tony. I'm just stuck with this useless bunch of twats.'

This produced even more laughter, so much so in fact that we couldn't carry on. Ever after the literacy group was known as 'the twats'. There were eventually eight in the group. No-one dropped out. The hook which kept them there was the relaxed atmosphere and the humour. When you're locked away year after year any diversion of whatever kind is craved. This is why there can be serious fights, protests or what have you in prison. Anything to break the dreadful grinding monotony.

5

About a year after we started the governor asked to see me.

'How's it going Jim?' Of course she knew already.

'It's going OK. I think the group is making progress.'

'And enjoying themselves?' Like I said, she knew exactly what was going on. She asked the prison officer to leave us.

'I've been looking through your file. You seem to have been behaving yourself both here and in Pentonville.'

'Trying.'

'How long have you got to do?'

'Not up to me, is it?' I was referring to the fact that a lifer is only released when the authorities say so, irrespective of the tariff.

'Ok, well your tariff was fourteen years. Which means if all goes well you'll be out in three. I'll certainly do my best to see that happens. At your trial you pleaded not guilty but since then you've acknowledged your guilt. So which is it?'

'Like you said, I've said I did it and expressed remorse.' That was the way the system worked – a classic Catch 22. If you were innocent and continued to maintain that innocence you would not get out. The system could not be wrong. She looked at me for a long time without saying anything, then:

'This is unofficial, between you and me, and goes no further, nothing on your record.' Another long pause.

'What do you want me to say?'
'I'd like to know the truth.'
'Why?'
'Curiosity. Despite my role, I am interested in people and their stories, and the truth.'
I told her the story of going to the house and finding Laura dead, my subsequent relationship with Alice and my revelation to her that had been my downfall.
'And there's something else.'
'Go on.'
'About a year after I went to prison I was notified that Alice wanted to visit. I had no idea why she wanted to see me but I felt I had nothing to lose by seeing her. Well I was wrong about that. It was a visit motivated by malice and it still astounds me that she could do what she did. That somebody could be so evil as to inflict such unnecessary suffering on someone purely out of sadistic pleasure, because that's what it was. It was bad enough that I was serving a sentence for something I didn't do but what she told me was really twisting the knife.'
'For goodness sake what on earth did she say to you?'
'She confessed that she had killed Laura.'
'Just like that?'
'Just like that. She must have felt that she was now immune from any chance of being held responsible but why come and tell me? As I say it can only have been out of hatred.'
'Did she tell you how it happened?'
'She and Laura were in a relationship. They were both bisexual It seems that Alice felt that Laura was paying too much attention to various men and not enough to her. They had a furious drunken row and Alice had thumped her with the decanter. She hadn't meant to kill her of course. She panicked and cleared out of the house. Fortunately for her, this idiot came along and left his fingerprints all over the place giving a plausible explanation for the killing to the police and letting Alice off the hook.'
'That's quite a story.'

'I got in touch with my brief about the possibility of it being used for my appeal but he dismissed it out of hand. He said that what she said to you doesn't constitute evidence.'
'No, I shouldn't think it does.'
'She said one more thing before she left. She told me that I would never find her so not to bother trying.'
'Well at least that was good advice. Any suggestion that you were trying to track her down that got through to the authorities and you would be back in here in no time. Well thank you for telling me that. As I said it will go no further. As far as the record is concerned you have admitted your guilt.'
'Are you finished with me?'
'Yes but I may want to see you again, when it gets warmer.'
'What about?'
'You'll see.'
I left mystified. When it gets warmer. What was she on about? When I did find out I could not have been more surprised.

*

I was back at the community library before it opened. At exactly 08.30 a woman of thirty or so accompanied by a small child arrived. She looked surprised to see me.
'Hello. You're keen.' She smiled, unlocked the door and went in. I followed.
'I hoped someone would be here. Would you just hold the fort for a minute while I pop Teddy to the nursery?'
'Yes but..'
'Won't be a minute. Help yourself to coffee.' She was gone.
I had a look round. Two walls were lined with books; another had a desk and chairs and a filing cabinet. In a corner were various cups, tea bags, instant coffee and a kettle. At the front window was a table with two chairs. I sat in the one that gave me the best view of No.17. A stout, elderly woman arrived and looked through the window. She came in. I had the feeling that I was about to have a disagreeable experience.
'Who are you?'

'Good morning. Same question to you.'
'Where's Carrie.' She didn't wait for an answer but walked to the back of the room. It wasn't long before she was back again. 'I usually sit there.'
'Well there's another chair next to mine. Perhaps you'd like to sit there.' She wandered off again and thinking I should justify my presence here, I took a book from the shelf behind me and pretended to start reading it. It was about gardening, a subject of little knowledge on my part, and less interest. Before I could get beyond the first page I saw some movement at No.17. A woman was coming out with two children. My heart was thumping. The old woman was chuntering on about something but I wasn't listening. At last, after all these years. But that wasn't her. This woman was dark and thickset, whereas Alice was tall and blonde. Had I got it wrong? Was my information out of date? The girls with the woman were both blonde. Maybe the woman was a friend or an au pair. She was quite young. I was clutching at straws, I knew. But to have come so far and still... I let the thought hang. I had intended to stay in the library a while, watch comings and goings but I felt so disappointed I just wanted to get out. The woman who I assumed must be Carrie arrived back just as I was leaving.
'Going already?'
'That nice lady wants my chair.' Carrie made a face. Clearly mine was not the first nose to be put out of joint.
'Won't you stay and have a coffee?'
I said that I might return later or tomorrow. Now what would I do? Everything had built up to this moment and I hadn't thought very much further. I didn't want to go back to the hotel so I thought I would take a look at the village. I walked back towards the station and then branched off on Mill Road. Nothing to see here, houses and then supermarkets, a petrol station. Mill Road led into Church Hill where, unsurprisingly, there was a church, St. John's. It seemed a large church for so small a village. It was constructed of flint and as I read, once inside, dated from the 15th century. Its interior wasn't at all like the church that I

remembered from childhood – gloom and hard pews. Here was brightness and comfort – padded chairs no less. I sat for a while, looking towards the strange, stained-glass windows. It was odd to be in such a large space and be alone. I sat for a long time and felt myself calming. Once more I questioned my motives for being here. What did I hope to gain? I was out. I had a chance to create some kind of life for myself. I had the saintly Colette in my life, though goodness knows why. As I sat there, quite happy, someone came in, a woman, the vicar clearly. She hesitated, not knowing whether to approach me or not. I turned to her and smiled.

'Are you alright there? I'm not interrupting your prayers, am I?'
I laughed. 'No prayers, just enjoying this lovely peaceful space.'
'And now I'm disrupting your peace.'
'I guess you're entitled to, seeing as who you are. But it's OK, I was just about to move on.'
'Only if you really want to. I wondered why you found this space so special. Is it a long time since you've been in a church?'
'Not since I was a child, but it's not that. It's a long time since I had so much space to myself. Before you ask - prison'
She said nothing.
'And now you're thinking am I trapped here with a dangerous lunatic.'
'Not at all, I…'
'It's alright I'm an entirely reformed character.'
'You must have been away for a long time.'
'Fourteen years, for murder.' I couldn't resist it. She flinched only slightly.
'Do you want to talk about it?'
'What's the point? It's all past and done.'
'You don't live here, do you? Why have you come to Saxmundham? Is it something to do with your crime?'
I was impressed. No fool this one. 'I'll tell you what vicar, if I feel the need to talk I'll come back, how's that?' In truth I felt an overwhelming desire to talk to her, to spill it all out, and maybe doing so would have purged me of the need to do

whatever I was going to do. But I didn't want to be purged. Not yet.

'That's fine, come and see me anytime.' I'll either be here or at the vicarage.

The church seemed to mark the end of the village. I carried on out into the country. Walking was not easy. There was no pavement and cars were passing all the time. I turned to see a bus coming. There was no bus stop but I put my hand out anyway and was surprised to see the bus stop.

I got on. 'Where are you going?' The driver seemed taken aback by my question.

'Leiston and then Thorpeness.' I bought a ticket to Thorpeness. I clambered to the top deck, where all alone I sat in the front seat. All the things I had not seen for so long were being presented before me in a panorama. Fields, farms, woods, a windmill, a tumbledown house. As we got nearer to Thorpeness the countryside changed. It became flatter. There was rough ground covered with gorse, a river and a lake and then, my God the sea! I had no idea Saxmundham was near the sea. How long since I had last seen the sea – twenty years? I got off the bus and walked to the beach. There was no-one and nothing there, just sea and sky. I could feel myself smiling at the joy of it all; the susurrating sea and the unending sky. And as I stood there I thought of that first time with Julia.

*

6

Only I didn't know her name then. I was called back to the governor's office one morning about two months after my last encounter with her.

'Would you like to go for a walk?' I just stared at her. What was she talking about?

'I mean outside.'

'I don't understand what you mean.'

'It's quite simple. If I can trust you to not abscond I will take you for a walk outside the prison. Now would you like that, yes or no?'

'Yes but where? What about my clothes?'

'I've got your civilian clothes here. We'll go to the common. You can change in here. I'll wait outside. Oh, and another thing, I don't want any other prisoners knowing about this.'

As we went out through security I felt as though the staff were looking at me in an odd way. This must seem very strange to them. Outside we got into the governor's car. I was finding it difficult to adjust to this seismic change in the immutable prison regime. The countryside near the prison was very pretty and I just gazed out the window at it. So much I had forgotten. After a while I recovered my senses enough to ask: 'Why are you doing this?' She waited a while before answering.

'I think you've had a very rough deal. I suppose I felt sorry for you.'

'There are a lot of blokes in there that have had a rough deal. Not necessarily that they are innocent but they've had a rough deal in life generally. Many of them had a bad start in life and never overcame it.'

'Do you think I don't know that?'

'Of course. It's your job. But the general public have no idea what prisons are like. What the people inside are like. I had no idea until I became one of them.'

We were at the common. She set off on a path and I followed. The common was quite bare at this point and I was struck by the immensity of the sky, stretching from horizon to horizon in a great circular sweep. In prison I only ever had sight of a rectangular segment of sky. This though, was something entirely different, almost intimidating. As we walked I stumbled a couple of times and felt disorientated.

'Are you OK?'

'Yes but this feels so strange.' Then I realised what it was. For more than ten years I had only walked on hard surfaces. Walking on soft ground was quite different. My feet had to bend this way and that to accommodate the unevenness of the surface I was walking on. I explained this to the governor, who laughed and remarked that such a thing had never occurred to her.

'There must be lots of strange sensations you're experiencing, emotions too.'

'Yes governor, and being near a woman is one of them.'

'Yes, and are you OK with that?

'Of course governor. It makes a nice change to get away from all that testosterone.'

She laughed. We walked on, conversation coming with some difficulty. We talked about family. She was an only child, once married, now divorced, no children, so she had very little family to talk about. It was strange to think of her as a person outside of the prison environment. But today everything was strange. We walked for about an hour describing a circle. I had forgotten so much. The way trees move in the wind, throwing the light back and forth on the ground; the sound of birds; the little spring flowers pushing through the turf, the names of which I had never known. All so new, but yet remotely familiar.

Back near the car there was a felled tree. I was quite weary, unaccustomed to even this modest level of activity. I sat and looked out at the trees and then without warning I was flooded with an access of emotion. Unable to help myself, I wept. I buried my face in my hands and let out great howling sobs. Julia walked a little way away and waited till it was over.

'It wasn't that bad, was it?' She made me laugh.

'I'm sorry about that but to see what I have missed all these years. All these things that are so ordinary but so wonderful.'

She said nothing and neither did I but I had the feeling that she was quite moved by my outburst. We sat in silence on the way back to prison, where I changed back into prison clothes and was taken back to my landing. I sat on my bed for a long time thinking about what had happened, trying to make sense of it, trying to deal with the emotions it had provoked. I realised that over the years I had become insulated from what had happened to me. I had accepted my imprisonment as normal. Today's experience had stirred the sediment that had settled to the bottom and now everything was cloudy. I was still sitting there when Gazzer came past. 'We're making up a poker game. You interested?'

'I don't think so, Gaz.'

'What's up, not like you to turn down a game.'

'I know, just feeling a bit low mate. Be alright tomorrow.'

'OK. You been outside? Looks like you caught the sun.'

'No, just having a hot flush. Must be on the turn.'

He laughed, content with my explanation, and went on his way. I hadn't thought about the sun. Everyone in prison has a rather unpleasant complexion, the well-known prison pallor, so somebody who has any kind of colour stands out. If there was to be a next time, and the governor hadn't ruled it out, I would need to be careful.

From that day on I found myself waiting to be summoned to see the governor again. It was on my mind all the time. My equilibrium had been well and truly disturbed. The call came two weeks later, another sunny day. The warder who took me down must have known what was going on but said nothing. Back with the governor again, she asked if I would like another walk. Of course I would, but I pointed out about the sun problem. Something else she hadn't thought about it. She thought she had an old straw hat in the boot that I could wear and so it turned out. We made the almost identical walk as the last time, conversation coming a bit more easily now, especially as we left the personal and talked about safer subjects. It seemed that we both had an interest in politics and philosophy. In fact I had an interest in almost everything, having devoured most of the library at both prisons. I think she was glad to be able to talk to someone at her own level. This was not to do with intelligence but more to do with having an 'informed' brain. What I lacked in experience of the world I made up for in my extensive knowledge gained from reading.

These excursions took place every two or three weeks, depending on her commitments and on the weather. I think it was on the fourth or fifth occasion that she asked me to call her Julia. That took some getting used to on my part. Whether it was on the fourth or fifth it was certainly on the occasion following that things took a turn for which I was quite unprepared. We were about half way round our circuit, passing through a little glade surrounded by trees. She stopped and turned to me. She put her hand on my arm and looked up at me.

'Do you find me attractive Jim?' Unprepared I was, but somehow unsurprised. A kind of intimacy had developed between us over the weeks, perhaps almost an attraction. Julia was at least ten years older than me, close to fifty I guessed, but still a handsome woman.

'Why do you ask me that?' I eventually replied. She cast her eyes down.

'So you don't, or you don't think it's appropriate that I should ask.' It was a statement, but a question nevertheless.

'Julia you are a beautiful woman but I'm a prisoner and you're the governor. So where does that question lead?'

She gave a little chuckle. 'I don't know. I suppose I want to feel attractive to at least one person. Not a lot to ask is it?'

'There must be a thousand men out there who find you attractive. Men far more suitable than me.'

'Would that it were so Jim. Perhaps you could pop out and round up a few of these thousand men because I haven't found any of them. Will you at least kiss me?'

We kissed, clumsily and briefly. I felt myself flush and apologised for my clumsiness.

'Practice makes perfect. Kiss me again. Shall we lie down?'

We did and kissed passionately. Her touch on my body was electric. She could feel my arousal. She unzipped me and mounted me. She had come prepared. Today she had worn a skirt with nothing underneath. It was all over in seconds. She lay on top of me and stroked my face. I turned my head away.

'Don't worry, that was inevitable after so long. It will be better next time.'

I turned back to face her. 'Next time? Julia you are committing professional suicide if this gets out. Bad enough that you are taking me outside the prison but this… Do you trust your staff?'

'So far, so good. But that's my worry not yours.'

We spent the rest of the walk in silence but she linked my arm and smiled up at me from time to time. I returned to my cell more confused than ever. I hadn't been long back when three of the lads came by.

'How's the governor's pet then?' This from Bluey.

'Very well thank you, and you?'

'What's this all about then, you going to see the governor all the time?'

'Well she looked at me and she must have thought I was the best shag in the prison so she drags me down there so I can give her one.'

'Ha, ha. Very funny. Some of the blokes think you're going down there to grass them up.'

'You're right of course. I've been telling her how the tunnel's been getting on.'

'The tunnel. Is there a tunnel? Why didn't I know about it?' Ivor was not the brightest button in the box.

'Ivor you fucking idiot. He's pulling your plonker. So Jim, what's it about?'

'It's just library stuff, the literacy group all that. She has to keep tabs on everything. What else would it be? There's fuck all to grass anyone up about. Apart from the tunnel.'

'Yeah the tunnel. Come on chaps. Let's see how it's getting on.' This was for poor Ivor's benefit, who was now more confused than ever. I'm pretty sure I was believed. There was in fact very little to grass anyone about. One or two of the blokes had managed to brew some hooch on a couple of occasions but that was about it. I doubt if the management would care, even if they knew. As I said before, the main aim of everyone on this wing was to do their time as comfortably as possible and that meant sticking to the rules, more or less.

Waiting to be summoned became a torture. Every time the weather looked like it might be fine I found myself listening for the footfall of the prisoner officer coming to collect me. It was more than three weeks before the next call came. The routine was as before. We always parked away from the main car park of the common, on a little patch of rough ground by the side of the road. We rarely saw anyone on our walks. Once or twice we saw dog walkers coming towards us and veered off the path to avoid meeting them. Julia didn't want to be recognised for obvious reasons but it seemed to me that the main danger to her would come from her own staff.

There was a tension between us and an unspoken question. As we neared the glade Julia, who had her arm through mine, started to press hard with her fingers. No sooner were we in our little dell than she turned to me and kissed me passionately. Her hands roved across my body and she drew me to the ground. There was something fierce about her love making, almost masculine in its urgency. She wanted me inside her straight away. She moved against me and within a very short time came to a climax. I was shocked but delighted. After a minute or so she started to move against me again and then it was all over for me too. We lay together for a while, she nestling her head against mine, planting little kisses on my hair, my cheek, my ear, and then rolled off and laughed. It was the laugh of a young girl.

'What's so funny?'

'Just thinking about the madness of all this.'

'Like I told you before, you're crazy.'

'I know Jim, and don't think I've got any silly romantic ideas. We both know what this is. At least I hope we do.' She looked at me.

'I have no complaints. My treatment in this prison has been exemplary.' She laughed. 'I will be happy to give you a reference for any future job application in the prison service.'

She laughed again, but a little forced this time, and the moment was over. We gathered ourselves together and headed back to the car. There were two more trips to the glade and then I heard nothing for more than a month, until one day Chas, one of the warders, as he was walking past me said: 'She's gone.' Of course I knew who he meant but feigned ignorance.

'Who's gone, where?'

'New prison, female only.' At which he laughed. It wasn't difficult to work out what had happened. One of her own staff must have put the boot in.

*

7

I walked along the beach towards the sun. The houses soon ran out and then it was just me and the sea. I felt a lightness and calm that had been alien to me for fourteen or more years. My journey to Saxmundham seemed to be having consequences that were both unimagined and just weeks ago inconceivable. First the church and now this. But this is what ordinary people experience all the time, the commonplace, the everyday familiarity of all possibilities. And as I thought about this the purpose of my trip seemed remote from me, as though it was another person that had travelled all this way to do what he knew not.

I made my way back to Thorpeness. There was a pub in the village and I thought I would get something to eat. The pub décor was the result of a designer's concept of what an eighteenth century pub might look like, though judging from the exterior the building was no more than sixty or seventy years old. Black beams, stone floors, brass and pewter pots on shelves had the effect of making the interior look unwelcoming and dingy. It came as no surprise to find the bar was occupied by only two women and a child, huddled in a corner over sandwiches. Or perhaps it was the landlord's demeanour which kept the customers away. A surlier looking expression would be difficult to conjure up. Perhaps he was so miserable because he had been lumbered with this awful manifestation of the pub designer's art.

But anyway it wasn't beyond him to supply a pint of beer and a decent looking sandwich. I retired to my own corner where I came under the gaze of the two women who had by now stopped talking, perhaps finding looking at me more entertaining than the things they were saying to each other. I had to remind myself once more that I wasn't wearing a suit with broad arrows or that in any other way it was clear that I was a released convict, but it took an act of will. After these few weeks it came as no surprise to me that so many ex-cons manage to manipulate themselves back inside. The outside world was as strange to me as the inside world had been fourteen years ago.

I wanted to get back to Saxmundham to check out Dalby's movements, if indeed he did travel by train to and from Ipswich. The bus timetable told me that I had a nearly two-hour wait so I decided to try my luck at hitching. I had barely positioned myself in what I thought was a good spot just outside the village and put my thumb out when a car stopped. In fact it was the first car to come along. The female driver leaned over, wound down the window and said the one word 'Saxmundham?' I confirmed her intuition monosyllabically and got in.

'You must be a mind reader. How did you know where I wanted to go?'

She laughed. 'Where else would you be going? You're not from round here.'

'How do you know that?'

'Because I'm the doctor that deals with Thorpeness and Leiston and I know everybody.'

'Are you from the area yourself?'

'No, I'm a Londoner but I've been here twenty years.'

'You must like it then.'

'It's a very pleasant place to live. Clearly you've never been before. What brings you here?'

'It's too long a story and I'm not sure I want to tell you.'

'Well, I know one thing about you.'

'Go on.'

'Being a doctor trains you to pick up clues about people. This isn't stuff you learn at medical school but it comes with experience. It's important because people often won't immediately tell you what is bothering them and you have to dig deeper. There are visual clues as well – your pallor for example and the clothes you're wearing. But there is something else. You're manner towards me changed after you became aware that I was a doctor. You became ever so slightly deferential.'

'I would have thought that most people were deferential towards doctors.'

'Used to be. Not now.'

'OK. I'm waiting for your revelation.'

'You've either been living abroad for a long while or you've been in prison.'

'That's very good but frightening too. I might as well still be wearing prison uniform.'

'Remember what I said. It's only through years of experience that I can work these things out. Most people would have no idea.'

'So bearing in mind what you've discovered aren't you worried that you're sitting next to an ex-con?'

'Strangely, no. I'm not sure why, maybe it's my doctor's instinct again.'

'So what would you do if I turned out to be a maniac, kidnapping you and your car?'

'It's interesting that you should ask that because I've often wondered why people in that situation don't do something to break the hold that this person has over them.'

'Do something like what?'

'Well you could deliberately bash into another car or perhaps wrench the wheel and turn the car over.'

'Why do you suppose that doesn't happen, then?'

'I think it's because people's thought processes become paralysed. Their only thought is to do as they are told and not antagonise the kidnapper.'

'So in that situation do you think you would be different?'

'Who can say? You're not going to test me out are you?'
I laughed. 'That would be rather bad manners after you've been kind enough to give me a lift.'
'You strike me as a man on a mission. A mission that's brought you here. Maybe something to do with your spell in prison. Revenge?'
I said nothing.
'You seem a likeable and intelligent young man but there's an anger in you. Think carefully. You've got plenty of years ahead of you. Are you going to do something you'll regret?'
By now we were sitting in the middle of Saxmundham. I continued to say nothing.
'I don't usually do this but here's my card. If you feel stuck you can give me a ring.'
I took the card and thanked her. The conversation had been unsettling. I found myself reluctant to get out of the car. Once again I had an urge to pour out my story, to receive support and consolation for the wrong that had been done to me. We sat there and she seemed in no hurry to get rid of me but I had to remind myself that I hadn't come to Saxmundham to confess. I thanked her once more and got out of the car. As I walked down the street I looked back and saw her staring after me. I was in turmoil again.

*

About six months before my fourteen years was up I came before the parole board. They asked me all the usual stuff about accepting my guilt, being remorseful, intending to live a quiet and sober life if released. It was merely going through the motions. They had all the information they already needed to make a decision. About two weeks later I received official notification of my release date on licence, subject to the usual provisos. I would have served just two weeks over fourteen years by then, which was 17 May 1990. It was not long after this that I was told I had a visitor. I could not imagine who it would be and certainly hadn't thought of Julia, for it was she. I was shocked by her appearance. She had clearly gone to some trouble. She wore lipstick and eye shadow and had on a pretty flowered blouse with a cream skirt but she looked terrible. She was thin and had dark shadows under her eyes. Neither of us spoke for a few minutes. Her eyes were misty when she finally broke the silence: 'How are you Jim?'

'I'm fine, but you…'

'I know, I've been unwell lately.' I didn't like to ask with what, and another silence ensued.

'I hear you're likely to be out before too long.'

'I don't even like to think about it, in case something goes wrong at the last minute.'

'It won't. You would have to do something pretty drastic for them to keep you in. Have you got any plans then?'

'No, I can't think further than the 17 May.'

'No-one to meet you. Nowhere you can stay?'

'I'll manage. Julia, why have you come?'

'Well just for that reason. You'd be surprised how many prisoners are back inside within a few weeks, days even. They have no money, nowhere to live. They commit a silly crime and bingo, banged up again. I don't want that to happen to you. I'm going to give you my address and phone number and I want you to contact me a soon as you get out.'

'Thanks.' I really didn't want to talk about this anymore. It seemed tempting fate to start making arrangements. I changed the subject. '

How's the new job going?' Another long pause.

'What do you mean?'

'The women's prison'

'I don't know what you mean. I haven't worked for the prison service since I left here.'

'One of the prison officer's told me that you had been transferred to a women's prison.'

'He was pulling your leg.'

'Oh Christ. So did they sack you?'

'Not exactly. An arrangement was come to and I took early retirement.'

'And that was because of…Someone squealed on you.'
'It would seem so.'
'I'm sorry.'
'Don't be. I knew what I was doing, the risk that I was taking.'
'I assume they just knew about the walks, not the…'
We both looked round at the prison officer who we hoped wasn't listening.
'No, not the…' We both giggled and it was good to see Julia smile. Even so I couldn't escape the feeling that she really was quite seriously ill.
She started to get up. 'Don't forget what I said.'
She looked over at the guard and then blew me a little kiss.

8

As the date of my release drew closer I found myself being cold-shouldered by most of the blokes on my wing. It wasn't unexpected. I'd seen this before. Someone close to release becomes no longer part of the world of inside. It's as though in the minds of the inmates he has already gone. There is nothing cruel or deliberate in this. It is the way men who have a long stretch to do, deal with the knowledge that it is not they who are leaving but someone else. They don't want to be reminded of the outside world, the world that is not theirs. I found myself becoming more and more anxious as the day approached. I couldn't say what was troubling me. Maybe I feared a last minute decision to keep me inside or perhaps it was a fear of the outside, an unknown world.

I hardly slept the night before and had been ready and dressed for hours when I was collected at seven o'clock. There were a number of formalities to be gone through, papers to be signed, my clothes and few possessions returned to me and my discharge grant handed out. I had seen a few of the lads the night before to say my goodbyes. I could not really call many of them friends, except perhaps those in the literacy group. But these were not men to show emotion and the usual valedictory greeting was 'right, so fuck off then'. I had a good relationship with some of

the warders and in seeing me off the premises I got the habitual
'stay out of trouble' or 'see you back in a few weeks then', said
with a smile, and really more appropriate for habitual thief than
a murderer.
The prison faced on to the High Street. There seemed only one
direction to go. The first phone box I came to had been
vandalised; somebody had cut through the cord. What benefit
accrued to them for that pointless act? I needed to phone Julia. I
had had no contact with her since her visit and just assumed her
invitation still stood but I couldn't just turn up. At the second
phone box I fumbled and lost my money. I had no more change.
I walked on along the High Street with its butcher's and book
shops, baker's and tea rooms. It seemed a pleasant, twee sort of
place. I felt that everybody was looking at me. Maybe they were.
Maybe they were accustomed to the sight and could recognise a
newly released prisoner. I found Station Road. I would get some
change there. At the booking office I presented my travel
warrant. 'What do I do with this?'
'You need to change that for a ticket.'
'I want to go to Wivelsfield. Is that on the way?'
'Yes but you're not supposed to break your journey there.
You're supposed to go straight through to London. Are you from
up the road?' He nodded in the direction of the prison. I agreed
that I was.
'Just pretend you didn't know the rules. I don't suppose anyone
at Wivelsfield will check your ticket.'
'OK. Can you give me some change?' He could and then said:
'Just take it easy, eh? You'll be alright.' And then he smiled at
me. I thanked him, took my ticket and change. I felt flustered
and confused. I needed to sit and think and found a bench. His
kindness had taken me aback. I felt close to tears. I'd been
holding back emotion for months, ever since I knew my release
date. I sat there for a while clutching my package to me like it
was a comfort blanket. After a while, calm returned and I sought
out a phone box. No answer. I waited a few minutes and tried
again. Same result. My plan, such as it was, was falling at the

first hurdle. I would just have to take a chance and go to her house. I checked out the trains. Lewes station was confusing – too many platforms going in different directions. I eventually found someone to ask.

It didn't take many minutes to get to Wivelsfield. No one checked my ticket there or on the train. Noel Rise wasn't difficult to find but it was one of those streets where the houses had names rather than numbers. The houses were detached and set back from the road. It made it difficult to read the names and I had to walk down some of the front paths to be able to read them. Attempted burglary, returned to prison, went through my mind. The seventh house on the left was Julia's, 'Rosedene'. There was indeed a rose on one side of the front door, with branches straggling across the doorway. It looked long unattended. The rest of the garden too bore the stamp of neglect. The flower beds were full of weeds and the lawn uncut. A bird table in the centre of the lawn on a rustic post had slipped sideways and seemed imminently about to detach itself from its support. The curtains were drawn in all the windows. It was now past ten o'clock. I knew Julia must be in, as her car was on the drive. That too had an air of neglect, even of abandonment. It was filthy and there was a long scrape along the offside, which was not new. The paint had come away and the metal had started to rust.

There was no point in just standing there. I rang the bell, no sound. I knocked, no answer. I waited and knocked again. After about three or four minutes I heard the sound of bolts being drawn back and the door opened. The Julia that stood there was almost unrecognisable. She was dressed in a nightgown over pyjamas. Her hair, almost completely grey, was matted to her scalp. Her eyes gleamed out from sockets that were black and sunken. Her face too had shrunk back on to her skull. She held a stick. Neither of us spoke. It was difficult to say who was the more shocked.

'Julia I...'

She turned away. 'You'd better come in.'

I followed her into the hall and into the sitting room. She lowered herself into one of the two armchairs by the fireplace, grimacing with pain. I stood in that dark room. I started several sentences in my head but before I could voice any of them she gestured to the mantelpiece. 'Get me those pills will you? I need a glass of water. Could you…?' She waved her arm towards the back of the house. The kitchen was another mess. Unwashed pots in the sink and on every surface. Opened food packets lying around; a half-eaten pie lay on a plate. I got her water and she took the pills.

'I have to take those three times a day. The pain…' She left it unfinished.

'Julia, I tried to…'

'It doesn't matter. You can't stay here.' That, I really didn't need telling.

'Julia, what's happened?'

'I've got a few months, possibly only weeks. I'm going into a hospice. My nieces will get this house. They'll want to sell it as quickly as possible, so you see you can't stay. What will you do?'

'I don't know exactly. I hadn't really got much further than coming here.'

'Pass me that pot will you, the one with the dolphins.' I did as she said.

'Look, there's at least two hundred pounds here. You'll need to find somewhere to stay.'

'Julia, I can't…'

'Don't be so bloody stupid. Money's no good to me and when I'm gone my nieces will get it and they've already got plenty. Well, you'd better get going and get yourself sorted out.'

'Yes, OK, and thank you.'

I went towards the doorway into the hall. She didn't follow. I looked back. 'Goodbye then.' She didn't look up or speak. I let myself out and slammed the door. I found it difficult to reconcile the Julia I had just seen with the woman who I had spent those moments with on the common. Although I knew of course of the devastating effects of wasting diseases this was the first time that I had been personally confronted with them. Mum and Dad had died while I was in prison and in the period of my life before prison I had known no-one else who had been seriously ill.

I walked back to the station. I had been given the phone number of an organisation that supposedly helped ex-prisoners. I hadn't reckoned on needing it but had hung on to it. A long ring was finally answered: 'Welfare service.'
'Hello, I wonder if you can help me. I've just been released and have nowhere to stay.'
'Shouldn't you have contacted us before your release?' was the somewhat unhelpful reply, delivered in an equally unsympathetic tone. Was I wasting my time?
'I thought I had accommodation sorted out but was let down at the last minute.'
'Ah, a not unfamiliar story. You're not the first. A lot of people think they want to help ex-prisoners only to find when faced with the reality that they are not quite ready.' This said somewhat more sympathetically.
'Where are you? We have addresses in different parts of the country where we can usually help people.'
'I'm on my way to London.'
'Yes, but where in London?'
'Well the train comes into Victoria.'
'OK. Well there's a hostel a couple of streets away from the station. You should have phoned them beforehand but they may be able to help you. I'll give you the phone number.'
'I'm sorry but I haven't got anything to write with.' Now I felt a bloody fool.
A sigh. 'The address is 24 Mount Street. Do you think you can remember that?'
'Yes, thanks.'
'If they can't help get back to us.' She rang off.
No-one checked my ticket at the station, on the train or at Victoria. I was to learn later what a sorry state the railways were

in. Cuts in staff meant that free travel was becoming the norm in some places, for those with little conscience or money. Victoria was heaving with people, all intently going somewhere. But where I wondered. Why weren't these people at work? The movement, the sound was overwhelming. I thought back to the ordered routine of prison. No wonder old lags found themselves drawn back so often.

Mount Street had tall Georgian houses along both sides. Most looked as though they were private homes but one or two had business signs in the window, although no indication of what the businesses were. 'Watson and Clark', 'Griffiths International Holdings', 'Roberts Brothers', I read. There was no sign at No.24. The exterior did not present an inviting picture. Paint peeled away from the stucco; the window frames showed bare wood in a couple of places, and a note on the door said: 'BELL NOT WORKING KNOCK'. I wondered what kind of flea pit I was getting into. I knocked. An electric catch released the door, which led into a small hallway. On the right was a part-glazed door through which I could see tables and chairs. On the left was an open door with a piece of cardboard stuck to the jamb on which was written in ballpoint 'Reception'. I walked in. In the far corner was a little counter on which sat a bowl of flowers. On the left under the front window was a leather sofa. A small table sat in the centre of the room on which was a vase of gladioli and some magazines. The room looked to have been freshly painted, a fact confirmed by a lingering odour.

'Hello.'

'I looked round.' A head appeared above the counter. The head belonged to one of the tiniest women I had ever seen. She must have been about fifty, dressed in a t-shirt and jeans, her brown hair cut short. She smiled, but not with her eyes.

'I was given this address by the EPW. I was hoping you might have a room.'

'We usually like people to contact us first but yes we've got a couple of rooms at the moment. The rooms are £30 a night and you get breakfast for that. There is no room service. You have to make your own bed, do your own cleaning. The bathroom is shared. There are some rules. The front door is locked at midnight. We don't allow visitors, of either sex. We are not prudes but experience teaches us that having friends in, of whatever kind often leads to trouble. No alcohol either. Do you want to look at the room?'

I did, and this diminutive, no-nonsense lady led me up. The room was very nice. Small but clean, a single bed to one side, a chest of drawers and a wardrobe on the opposite wall and a sink in the corner next to the window. A glance at the ceiling coving told me that this was a much larger room which had been sub-divided.

'Yes, that'll be fine.'

'How long do you think you'll be staying?' Since I had no idea, I failed to provide an answer.

'Look, give me rent for three days while you sort yourself out. If you want to stop less than that I'll give you your money back. If you want to stay longer you must tell me the morning after your last paid night. Breakfast is served between seven and eight. It's cereals and toast. We don't have the means to cook anything.'

I handed over the money.

'I'm Jean by the way. When you come back down I'll get you to fill in a form. Anything you think we can help with please ask. We don't have a sitting room but you can always come down and sit in reception if you're feeling a bit lonely.' This time she smiled with her eyes too.

9

I sat on the bed. So this is freedom, this little room in Central London. I stood up and looked out of the window. The view was of the back of the houses in the next street. The house immediately opposite had a ground floor extension, which made a terrace for the first floor, where French windows gave access. On the terrace were four people sitting at a table. There were plates and bottles – a lunch I supposed. The people were talking, by turns leaning forward, throwing their heads back, waving their arms. Quite drunk no doubt. These no doubt were the well-heeled middle class; people with good jobs, status, friends. And this is what I might have had - big house, decent income, family, children, nice friends. Instead I was an ex-con, destitute, homeless, jobless, friendless. The contrast with my neighbours couldn't have been greater and I felt a new wave of bitterness, like bile rising up in my throat.

I needed to phone the prison. They needed my address so that a probation officer could be assigned. I didn't fancy using the pay phone in reception. I didn't want everyone knowing my business. As I came downstairs Jean popped out: 'Everything alright?'

I confirmed that it was.

'Do you want to leave your key with me? We find it's better that way. A lot of you chaps seem to lose your key when you're out and about.' She wasn't finished with me. 'Do you need any clothes?' I thought she was going to fish out a bag of cast-offs. 'Only if you do, there's a clothes shop near the station that will give you a discount, if you mention my name. The owner's called Sam. I expect you'll want the labour exchange too. That's in Endlebury Street. It's not far from Sam's.'

It amused me that she used a name that hadn't been current for thirty years or more. I thanked her and handed over the key. She was right about the clothes. I looked like a better class of scarecrow. I set off for the station and remembered that she hadn't given me the form. Clearly it was of no great importance. She seemed to be an extraordinarily trusting person and perhaps that was the only way to be with the kind of people she had to deal with. People just out of prison might have found it hard to deal with anything that still resembled prison. Yes there were rules but they were not unreasonable. Her sex and her size were an advantage. No decent man likes to think that he would take advantage of someone weaker than himself, especially a women, though plenty do of course.

The prison asked me to ring back the following day to get details about my probation officer. Next was Sam's. The person I took to be Sam lurked behind a rail of clothes at the back of the shop. He was short, stout, and bespectacled. He had a remarkably greasy complexion, bald but for a few tufts of hair clinging to the scalp above his ears. There were clothes on rails everywhere. I wandered between them. I was shocked at the price of everything. My £200 wasn't going to go very far. Sam, if it was him, sidled up to me. 'One of Jean's boys?'

'Is it that obvious?'

'I get a lot of you boys in here. It's not difficult to tell. Come with me.' He took me to the back of the store. 'Look, everything on this rail is half price. They're discontinued lines. They're half price and I'll give you another 10% as well.'

I could see why no-one had bought these clothes. The styles and colours were mostly awful but I managed to find myself a pair of jeans in the right size and a couple of shirts. I needed a jacket but they were all too expensive. Sam saw me looking longingly at a rail of bomber jackets. 'Bit too pricey for you?'
'Unfortunately.'
'Tell you what, choose one. You can pay me when you get a job.'
'What? That's very kind but how do you know you'll see me again?'
'I don't. Listen, I've got two boys. Michael, the youngest was a bit of a tearaway in his teens. He eventually did a stretch for hot wiring and stealing a car. It was only six months but it really shook him up. He had a tough time inside. Some of the stories he told me had me in tears. He's straight as a die now, married, kids but he's never forgotten that time and neither have I. So when I knew Jean was opening up the hostel I thought I could help out a bit.'
'Have you known her long?'
'She's the sister of our old next door neighbour. She was often round there so that's how we got to know her. Heart of gold.'
I thanked Sam and wandered back to the hostel. Jean was there to greet me. 'Been to Sam's then?'
'Yes, what a nice man. I'll just park these and get round to the labour exchange, as you call it'
My visit to the labour exchange, now as I saw, called the Job Centre, was much as I expected. After a half-hour wait I was given an appointment for two days hence. It was after five o'clock and I hadn't eaten all day. I needed somewhere cheap to make my money last. There were lots of places round Victoria station but when I looked at the prices I could see they were not for me. What had happened to all the greasy spoons? I eventually found a place that wasn't too expensive and settled for a fry-up and a cup of tea.

With nothing much more to do on what was a bright and pleasant evening I thought I might take the first steps in trying to track down my nemesis. Our new house, the one that I never moved into, was out at Southgate. I could remember the address even now and thought it wouldn't be difficult to find again. I knew she was no longer there but felt it was possible she might have left a forwarding address or at least given some indication of where she was going. I took the Victoria line to Finsbury Park and changed to the Piccadilly. Chase Way was a street of 1930s semis, not far from the station. I remembered the route but it looked different to how I remembered it. Some of the front gardens had been paved over to provide parking. It was not attractive. The street that I remembered had well-tended gardens and what few cars there were, were parked on the road. I walked along to No.14. I started to become nervous but for no reason. She was certainly not there and all I was doing was making a perfectly reasonable and innocent enquiry. When I got to No.14 for some reason I became uncertain that I had got the number right. Was it in fact No.18? I seem to recall there were two houses near to each other on sale at the same time. I walked along to No.18 to see if its appearance would jog my memory. It didn't. Which should I try first? I walked back to No.14 and stood looking at it. A lot could change in fourteen years. There was someone at the front window watching me. I was loitering, even if it wasn't with intent, so I thought I'd better get a move on. I walked down the path and rang the bell. It was a long time before the door was opened, by which time I was even more nervous. A woman, I guess in her late fifties, held the door open a crack. It was on a chain. She didn't look happy.
'Hello. I'm sorry to trouble you. I'm trying to get in touch with someone who used to live here. I wondered if you might have a forwarding address for her.'
'What do you mean? No-one's lived here.'
'It was a long time ago. She bought the house in 1976. I expect you bought it from her.'

'That's impossible. We bought the house in 1976.' As she said this she looked out towards the road. A car had drawn up and I didn't need to turn round to see who it was. Now she opened the door fully as two police officers came down the path.
'Alright luv. You gave us a call. What's the problem?'
'This man has been walking backwards and forwards looking at the houses. I was worried he was up to something.'
'What's he said to you?'
'Something about a forwarding address.'
I felt it was time to contribute my two pennyworth. 'I was trying to get the address of someone I thought used to live here. It seems I was wrong.' They took me back to the car. By now I was shaking uncontrollably.
'You alright?'
I thought it best to be completely honest with them. 'I just got out this morning – on licence. I'm terrified about going back inside for nothing. All I was trying to do was to track down an old friend. It seems I got the wrong house.'
'What were you in for?'
'Murder. No good telling you I didn't do it.'
They took my details an advised me about my behaviour. I was mighty relieved they took it no further. I walked back to the station on very unsteady legs. What did it mean? Had Alice decided not to buy the house after all? It seemed there were two possibilities. Either I had got the number wrong and it was No.18 or she had decided not to go through with buying the house and those people had stepped in, which meant she must have stayed at Tenterden Road. But how could I be sure? I dare not go back to Chase Way. When I arrived back at Mount Street I felt exhausted. Hard to believe that I had only been released that morning. Jean was there with the key.
'Everything all right?'
I confirmed that it was, even though I still felt decidedly shaken up. I was starting to think that I had been very lucky to be directed to Mount Street, and this kind woman. In fact, if I thought about it I had received little but kindness on my first day

out. First the booking clerk at Lewes, Jean at the hostel, and then Sam at the clothes shop. I sat on the bed and thought about my day, what it all meant, where I was going. Leaving prison I had had only two thoughts; the first that I would stay with Julia, the second that I would track down Alice. Well my plans had fallen apart upon first contact with reality. In truth, calling them plans was rather to flatter them. I would be forty next birthday. It didn't make sense to be obsessing about the past when I did at least have some future ahead of me. The problem was it was proving to be impossible to imagine what that future might be, other than a life of friendless, hopeless, poverty. And the anger towards Alice never seemed to diminish, and the compulsive need I felt to satiate that anger. Across the way the French windows were open. The sound of laughter and raised voices drifted out. Well they certainly liked to party, whoever they were. Once again I felt that bitter envy. But this was no good. I should get some sleep and see what the morning brought.

*

10

By the time I left the good doctor it was time for me to be heading to the station. The next part of my plan was predicated on a number of assumptions. Firstly that the Mr and Mrs Dalby that I had tracked down were in fact Alice and her husband. Secondly that Dalby worked in Ipswich. This second assumption was based on the fact that there would be little employment in such a small place as Saxmundham. However it was quite possible that Dalby worked from home or in some other town or was rich enough not to work. He might also drive to work by car. That of course was the third assumption; that he travelled from Ipswich by train. I had checked the train times and it seemed to me that the first train he might arrive by was the 17.53. I would have to follow anyone heading to Saxon Road hoping they would end up at No.17.

About a dozen people got off the first train. Three men headed in the right direction. I followed. One turned off right almost immediately. The other two carried on past Saxon Road. No luck. The next train from Ipswich came in at 18.25. Just two men headed in the right direction. One headed past Saxon Road but the other turned in. Was this him? He seemed about the right age, smart, good looking chap, the sort I could imagine Alice going for. But he continued down the even side of the road. Back to the station. I was starting to give up hope. If it turned out that

Dalby didn't come home this way, the plan that I had conceived would have to be abandoned and I would have try something else. The last thing I wanted to do was to knock on the door and have it slammed in my face, have the police called and be sent back to prison. This is why I needed a more oblique approach. There was another train at just past seven. Surely my last chance. Just one man headed in the right direction. He was quite short, rounded, balding, rosy cheeks, about fifty I thought. Surely not, but he headed into Saxon Road and crossed over to the odd side, and yes went into No.17. Well, not at all the person I imagined. But at least I could now put my plan into action. However, I still didn't know if he was the right person. Was he Alice's husband? I needed to see her. I would return to the community library in the morning hoping for a sighting.

I returned to the Bell. I needed to eat and more than that I needed a drink. A sandwich and a pint saw me settled into a corner. Two women came in, both about my age. One was short and blonde, the other tall and dark. They got their drinks and settled nearby. The blonde, who had her back to me, obviously had a story to tell, which I could tell from the cadences of her voice, alternately raised in outrage and lowered in confidentiality. While this was going on, the dark one threw the occasional glance in my direction. I felt embarrassed, not knowing where to look. I realised that my emotional development so far as human contact was concerned had become stunted by my incarceration. In my head I was still a 25 year old. I had never grown up. Things got worse when the blonde went to the loo and darkie now smiled at me. I felt the flush rising up my cheeks. I wished I had a book or something else to bury my head in. The blonde returned and shortly turned to look at me. I smiled at them both and raised my glass to them. A couple more minutes and the blonde came over. Oh God! What was going to happen now?

'My friend wants to buy you a drink.'

'Oh, does she. I well I…' I stuttered

'What are you drinking?'

'Bitter, but why don't I…'

She didn't wait for the rest of whatever I was going to say, which was just as well, as the words had yet to be formed in my brain. They both went to the bar, came back with the drinks and sat with me. Maybe my ideas of how women should behave were still lodged in the past but this seemed very forward to me. Anyway, now they were with me I actually felt more relaxed.

'I'm Sharon and this is Lucy.' This from the blonde.

'How do you do? I'm Jim.'

'Not seen you round here before.' Sharon waited for a response.

'No I'm just up from London. Business. You both from Saxmundham?'

'I am. Lucy's from Rendham. It's a little village.'

The conversation continued in this desultory fashion until Sharon finished her drink, got up and told Lucy she would see her in the morning. All carefully arranged, and the more I drank and the more I looked at Lucy, the more I liked the arrangements. Lucy was tall and slim, and very pretty. We sat in silence for a while. We both knew where this was going.

'You don't need to get home?'

'No, no rush. What about you? Are you staying here?' I agreed that I was.

'Is this a regular thing of yours, you and Sharon?'

'Yes, it's my husband's darts night. He doesn't get home till late so I like to get out myself.'

'I looked at my watch. What time do you have to get back?'

'Not for ages.'

She had finished her drink. I asked if she would like another. She said no and stared at me, pupils dilated.

'Perhaps you'd like to see my room.' I laughed as I said it and Lucy joined in.

'Love to.'

She took my arm as we went upstairs, giggling. Lucy wasted no time stripping off. She had a lovely lithe, muscle-defined body. There were no preliminaries, no tender foreplay. It was animal sex, and quite delightful.

The first time we spoke was as we lay there after.

'What time do you have to get back?'
'Not for ages. He's always late.'
'You don't sound too chuffed about him.'
'It's not just darts, there's quiz night, pool night, and every other goddamn night.'
'Spends a lot of time at the pub then.'
'Practically lives there.'
'So what's that all about? How long have you been married?'
'We've actually been together for fifteen years and the first twelve were great.'
'So what went wrong?'
A long silence.
'Three years ago Ken was involved in an accident. Not his fault. A little boy ran out into the road. Ken had no chance to stop. The boy was killed instantly. You can't imagine what it was like. The police investigation, the inquest. It went on for months. Even though the police actually said it wasn't his fault he just couldn't get over it. Started to drink and then got done for drunken driving, which meant he lost his job as a rep.'
'That's a terrible story. Have you got children of your own?'
'No, and that's what makes it worse. We can't have children, Ken's infertile.'
'So is he working now?'
'He's got a job as a packer in a warehouse. Half the money he was on before.'
'Does he know about your 'nights out'?'
'Yes, and he couldn't care less. We haven't had sex for three years. Don't get me wrong. I don't go shagging every time I go out. But I rather fancied you.'
'My lucky day.'
'And mine.'
With that Lucy started to get dressed. She left without any fond farewells or promises to meet again. A simple goodbye sufficed, for both of us. It took me a long time to get to sleep that night.

11

And in the morning I was still faced with my 'mission', whatever it might be. If I had reflected then, I might have said to myself: 'you're never planning more than one day ahead; is that a good way to lead your life?' But I didn't reflect and I didn't say anything to myself. I just carried on as before. I was at the community library before 08.30. Carrie arrived with Teddy as before.

'Hello again. Would you mind…? And she was off. I heard Bert before I saw him, an awful hacking cough coming down the road. A man of seventy or so came into the library still coughing. 'Carrie not here?'

'Just popped Teddy to the nursery.'

'I wondered if she's got my budgerigar books.' He looked at me as though I might know the answer. I thought but didn't say, with a cough like that you shouldn't be going anywhere near birds. Maybe he already had psittacosis. I really didn't want to get involved in this conversation. I wanted to keep a look out for activity at No.17. Bert came and sat in the chair next to me, held out his hand and told me his name. I barely looked at him.

'Waiting for someone?'

'No, just watching the world go by.'

'Hah, not much world going by here.' I wished Carrie would come back and give him his books. He was starting to annoy me.

71

But there she was. It must be her. Tall blonde with two little blonde girls. My stomach flipped. She passed by on the opposite side. She was in animated chatter with the girls, smiling and laughing. She hadn't changed. Still that erect posture, head upright, no fear of the world, a few lines maybe but very much the same person. I wondered if she would recognise me as easily as I her. I got up to go. Today would be the day I would put the plan into action. I hadn't noticed that Bert was speaking to me.
'Sorry Bert, I didn't catch what you were saying.'
'I said are you interested in budgerigars.'
'I don't know the first thing about them.'
'Well why don't you come with me and learn something?'
I laughed. 'Alright, but we'll have to wait till Carrie gets back.'
Who at that moment appeared, and before Bert could even get the question out, gave him his answer.
'No Bert, your books haven't arrived. You only ordered them two days ago.'
'Alright, I'll try next week. You coming?' This to me.
What else did I have to do all day except learn about budgies. We set off down Saxon Road, took a right and a left, which I noticed was taking us out of the village and just before we came to open country we arrived at a little cottage on the left. The kind of cottage that foreigners imagine everyone in England lives in. It wasn't thatched but had every other attribute of the English country cottage. It was in brick with a slate roof, double fronted with a small front garden. The garden was very neat, the borders planted with several different types of flowers, the only ones I recognised being pansies. There were roses growing up the front of the house. Bert pushed open the front door, which was not locked. He took me through to the kitchen. As we walked through the hall I glanced into the living room. Everything looked neat and tidy, the kitchen too, so I was surprised when I asked if his wife had gone shopping to be told that she had died five years previously. We went out the back door of the kitchen into a back garden as neat as every other part of the house. On the left a lawn with borders and on the right rows and rows of

vegetables. At the end of the path was a large shed with windows, which were wide open. Bert took me through a door and there they were, dozens of them in a huge cage. They seemed to get more excited at the sight of Bert. He put some seed into their feeders. They were of a multiplicity of shades of yellow, green and blue.

'Do they breed?' I asked.

'You bet. But it's a funny thing if you put just a male and female in a cage together they won't mate. You have to a have a bunch of them before they start mating.'

'Why's that?'

'In the wild they live in flocks, so if there's just two of them it's unnatural. They get stressed so they won't mate. Anyway, expect you've seen enough. Fancy a cup of tea?'

Before I had the chance to answer in the affirmative to both, Bert led the way back up the garden. I think he knew that I wasn't particularly interested in his budgies. Inviting me here was just a way of gaining some company. He sent me through to the living room while he made the tea. I wasn't expecting a full tea service but that's what Bert arrived with. Teapot, milk jug, sugar bowl and two cups and saucers. I could not remember the last time I had a seen a saucer. Use of a strainer implied that this was real tea, rather than bags. As if he had read my thoughts Bert confirmed that it was.

'Can't stand those bags. That's not a proper cup of tea.'

I could not fault Bert's tea, the best I'd had in a very long time.

'Bert you look after yourself very well. I couldn't help noticing how clean and tidy everywhere is, even the garden.'

'Couldn't live in a pigsty. I let things go a bit when Elsie went but then my daughter came round one day and gave me a rocket. Dad, she told me, that part of your life's finished but you're not, and you mustn't let yourself fall apart, think about me and David and the grandkids. She was right of course. I had a lot to live for but it gets terrible lonely sometimes.'

'You lived here a long time?'

'Since 47, when we got married. We rented this off the farmer and when he died his family let us buy it. That was in 1952, £400 we paid. Seemed a fortune then.'

'What was your work?'

'Before the War I used to work for a firm of seedsmen. They sold everything beside seeds; fodder, fertilisers, gates, all kinds of metal goods. I had a horse and cart and used to go round all the farms delivering the stuff. In those days a lot of the farms still used horses. There were some tractors but they were expensive and unreliable, so the old boys preferred to keep with their horses. Everything was slower then. There was always time for a chat. Every week I would go down to the station to pick up what we'd ordered. They would shunt a wagon into a siding and I would unload it on to my wagon. It would take me five or six trips to get it all. You can't imagine it now. Then the War came along. I ended up in North Africa in a tank, then Italy. Saw a lot of my mates killed. Terrible thing, a tank when it was hit. Went up like a bonfire. After the war they gave me my job back. A woman had been doing it. She wasn't best pleased. By then she was driving a lorry. I was alright because I'd been driving tanks. I still had to take a test though. That's how I met Elsie. She'd been a Land Girl up from Ipswich, working on one of the farms. They'd kept her on because she was good with the horses. I used to see her on my rounds. Things were never the same after the War though. A lot of the old boys died and the farms got bought up, got bigger and bigger. No time for a chat now. Some of the bigger farms ordered their stuff direct from the suppliers, cutting us out. I was lucky to keep my job up to retirement. Soon after I retired the firm went out of business. Yes, that world that I knew; that's all gone.'

I enjoyed listening to Bert. It made me realise how much I had missed talking to 'normal' people, I mean other than prisoners. It seemed to me that people like Bert were the backbone of Britain. Just getting on with life, uncomplaining, believing that being honest, doing your duty was the right thing to do. They didn't think too much about whether they were exploited or not, conservative in nature whatever they voted. Bert offered me another cup of tea but it was time to move on. He told me I could call in any time. I wondered had I made a new friend? I walked back into town on the search for something to eat. I came across Zorba's kebab shop. I had no idea what a kebab was but the prices displayed in the window seemed about my level so I want in. It turned out that a kebab was slices of mutton in a kind of bread roll with various vegetables. It was rather good.

I was starting to like Saxmundham. It was a pleasant little town and people were friendly. Zorba, if that was his real name, had given me a free drink, because 'you are first customer of day'. I wondered when the novelty of these experiences would wear off, experiences which for everyone else were just normal. I was in reality no more sorted out than the day I had left prison. It was still difficult to think clearly about anything. I had my 'mission', ill-defined as it was, and somehow I seemed to need to cling to it to give my life some structure. While having these thoughts I found myself, perhaps not coincidentally, walking once again along Church Hill. With an afternoon to kill I thought I might spend some time in the peaceful space of the church once more. As I came in I saw the vicar up near the altar with another woman, evidently the cleaner. They both turned to look at me but quickly turned back to continue their conversation. The cleaning woman finally turned away and set off down the aisle, clattering her way with her mop, broom and bucket to somewhere at the back of the church. Meanwhile the vicar too had disappeared. I closed my eyes and bowed my head. It was quiet now and as I sat I experienced once again a feeling of tranquillity. In prison there is never any peace. Even at night there are still the ordinary sounds of people asleep, as well as the tormented sounds of those crying out in their nightmares. Always the same people, quite normal in the daytime, but going through goodness knows what in their dreams.

I think I must have fallen asleep because when I heard a movement near me I was startled. I opened my eyes and looked up, unsurprised to see the vicar smiling at me.

'Come to me all ye who are heavy laden.' This said in an inquisitorial tone.

'You think I'm heavy laden.'

'Well, from what you've told me previously I think you must be.'

'Maybe. It's nice here. It makes me feel tranquil, peaceful'

'You think it's just the building?'

'You're not going to tell me it's God's doing.'

'I might think so, but you clearly don't. Not a believer?

'I don't wish to offend you but why should I believe in that fairy story when I don't believe any others?'

'We often have these kinds of discussions with our youth group and it always turns out the same way – faith is a matter of faith. There's not much more to say.'

'No I can see that. But I don't think you particularly want to discuss religion with me, or do you?'

'I would be happy to but I think you may something else on your mind, more pressing. Would you like a cup of tea?'

I agreed that I would and I was led by Angela, as she insisted I must call her, into the vestry.

'I'm Jim, by the way. I guess your name must mean something religious.'

'It means messenger of God.'

'Do you think your parents knew that?'

'Oh yes, they were deeply religious, my mother particularly.'

'They must be very happy that you've become a vicar.'

'Well actually I'm not exactly a vicar. I was elected by the congregation of this church to be their minister but I cannot perform the offices of the church. We have to get someone from a neighbouring church to do that. We're hopeful that within a few years the church will see sense and allow the ordination of women.'

'Good job I didn't ask you to hear my confession then.'

'Do you want to confess?'

'I haven't done anything yet.'

'Which brings us full circle. Your reason for coming to Saxmundham.'

'And what do you think that is?'

'I'm assuming it's connected with your conviction for murder.'

'A murder I didn't commit.'

'What's the connection with Saxmundham?'

'Well, the person who framed me for the murder lives here.'

'And now you've come to confront him, carry out your revenge, is that it?'

I wasn't about to let Angela know that we weren't talking about a man. This was a small place and she probably knew a fair few of the village's population. I didn't want to give her any clues to Alice's identity.

'The thing is I don't know what I want to do, what I might do. I just know I've got to see him. I'm never going to rest easy while he lives here in peace and comfort and I'm condemned to a life of poverty and disgrace.'

'Why should you have such a life?'

'Angela, you're not being real. Do this for me. Go outside on to Church Hill. Stand there and use your imagination to convince yourself that you have no home, no job, no friends, no family, that you are destitute, that you can be recalled to the misery of prison at any time for any reason without any kind of hearing, and you have no hope that anything will ever change for the rest of your life. Just try it.' Of course my life wasn't like that currently, thanks to Colette, but it might well have been and could be at any time.

There was a long silence.

'You're right. I've been a bit stupid. I've always thought I was able to see things from the other person's point of view but clearly I wasn't doing that in your case.'

Another long silence ensued. I had got myself a bit worked up and I was sorry I had become so angry with the vicar. She struck me as a decent sort of person, anxious to help but not knowing how to. It was she who spoke first.

'Am I forgiven?' I nodded assent. 'Which leaves where we are now, I mean where you are. From what you say, whatever action you take towards this person is liable to send you back to prison.'
'Are you going to tell me to forgive and forget?'
'I'm not going to tell you anything but the fact that you mention forgiveness suggests that the thought might have crossed your mind.'
'No, you're wrong. I cannot forgive, and every day of my life I'm reminded of my situation so I cannot forget. My problem is that this wrong that was done to me has been burning me up for fourteen years and will continue to do so until I have some kind of resolution.'
'I've been no help to you at all, have I?'
'Actually you have, if only allowing me to let off some steam. And it's good to feel your kindness.'
'Now you're embarrassing me.' We both laughed, happy to take some of the tension out of the air. I took my leave of the vicar, who once again told me that she would be there to listen or advise if I felt that that was what I wanted.

I walked back to the Bell. To put my plan in action I needed to check out and collect my stuff. It was still too early for Dalby's train but since I had nothing else to do I would go and wait at the station. Settling my bill left me with very little money. I could perhaps have afforded one more night but that would be it. I found a bench at the station and waited. There he was, on the same train as last night. I let him get a little ahead as he walked down Albion Street.
'Excuse me, I'm trying to find Saxon Road. Am I going in the right direction?'
Dalby turned to look at me, 'that's where I'm going.'
We walked on a little further.
'What number are you after?'
I fished in my pocket for the piece of paper, though of course I knew the number by heart.
'Number seventeen.'

'That's my house.'
'You must be Mr Dalby. I'm an old friend of Alice. Been trying to track her down for years. What a coincidence that I should ask you.'
'Have you just got off the train?'
'Yes, came up from London this afternoon.'
'I suppose your one of Alice's old London friends then. I'm sure she'll be pleased to see you. Since moving here we seem to have been a bit short of friends.'
We were at the door and my heart was beating so hard I felt it was trying to burst out of my chest. Dalby let himself in and his two little girls came running into the hall, grabbing his legs. The smallest said, 'mummy's making you a curry banana.'
Her sister, so much wiser, said, 'she means a car banana.'
Dalby laughed, 'Sounds interesting.' He called out, 'Alice I've got a surprise for you.'
'She came through from the kitchen smiling. When she saw me, the smile remained fixed to her face, but the colour left it.
'Hello Alice. Been a long time.'

*

_12_

I was only just in time for breakfast. Despite my inner demons I must have slept well, although when I woke I had no idea where I was. For one awful moment I thought I was back in Pentonville. The indefatigable Jean was there in the breakfast room.

'Bread there, toaster over there, cereals here, milk in the fridge. Can I make you a cup of tea?'

'Jean you're just amazing. I hope I get some money soon as I don't fancy leaving here. You're a real tonic.'

'Nothing from the labour exchange then?'

'Seeing them tomorrow. Jean you realise you're about fifty years out of date. It's called the Job Centre now.'

'Daft name. Probably haven't got any jobs.'

'At any rate none for me.'

'What you got on today then?'

'Got to find out about probation this morning, then tea with the Queen this afternoon.'

'I wouldn't bother. It'll just be a teabag.' We both laughed.

When I got through to the prison I was told that I had an appointment for that afternoon with a Mr Rawlings at the probation office in Buckingham Palace Road. The prospect of a free morning led my thoughts to Tenterden Road. Would I find there the information I needed? Tenterden Road was like a different place to the one I remembered. The front garden of every house had been paved or concreted over to provide hard standing for cars and many of the houses had had an extension put into the roof making them three-storey. The whole street looked much more affluent. Walking along towards number thirty-three I began to feel rather nervous, though I couldn't say why. Was it memories of the night I found Laura, or of my arrest, or did I feel there was something illicit in my purpose? By the time I arrived outside the house I was shaking. I walked on past, trying to tell myself that I was engaged in an entirely innocent task. Maybe it was the thought of the potential malevolence behind this 'innocent' task that was shaking me up. I walked to the end of the road and then turned back. I rang the bell. The sound of hoovering stopped and presently a young woman opened the door. A little girl clung to her legs and looked up at me. I put on a smile.

'Sorry to trouble you but I'm trying to get in touch with someone who used to live here. I wondered if you might have a forwarding address for them. The name was Travis, Alice Travis.'

'We do have a forwarding address but that doesn't sound like the name I remember. Do you want to come in for a minute, while I look to see what I've got?'

She showed me through to the living room. It was very strange to step over that threshold and even stranger to see that same purplish light once again. In fact it was a shock.

'I see you've got my old friend's aquarium.'

'Yes the people that we bought the house from had been left it by the previous people. They didn't want to take it so they left it for us. I'll just pop upstairs. All the papers are up there.'

The layout of the room was much as it had been when Alice and I had lived there. The fish tank still in the same corner, a sofa opposite the fireplace and armchairs either side. Along the wall opposite the window was a bookcase. I walked over to take a look. Most of the books seemed to be about engineering.

'Those are my daddy's books.' This from the little girl who had
remained with me.

'Are they? And what does your daddy do?'

'He makes tungles.'

Before I had a chance to find out what 'tungles' were the woman
returned with a large file of papers.

'I know we've got it here somewhere. My husband would know
where it was but he's away at the moment.'

'Making tungles.' I suggested.

She laughed. 'He's working on the Channel tunnel. We only get
to see him at weekends. Here it is. It's not the name you said.
The people we bought it from were called Baker. They moved
down to Kent. I remember the man saying it was for his work,
something to do with mining.'

'I didn't know there were mines in Kent but if you could let me
have that address, they perhaps will have an address for my
friend.'

She wrote it out for me, I thanked her and left. The address was
in a place called Aylsham. It would mean a trip to Kent but I was
running short of money and wouldn't be able to go unless the
Job Centre came up with something. My immediate concern was
my probation appointment that afternoon. To save money I
walked all the way from Tenterden Road to the probation office.
I was once again struck by how unfit I had become. By the time
I got to my destination I was feeling decidedly weary. I was far
too early for my appointment so I spent a while wandering the
streets near Victoria. Being in London again was like being in a
different city to the one I had known. I would not have believed
so much could change in the time I was 'absent.' The London of
pubs and cafes had become the London of wine bars, bistros and
bustle. All these people in a hurry to get somewhere. I asked
myself why weren't they at work? Where could they all be
going?

Mr Rawlings turned out to be a man in his mid-twenties, smart
suit and slicked back hair. He wanted to know what I was doing
about finding work. I told him about my Job Centre

appointment. He wanted to know what work I had done previously and when I told him agreed with me that there was little chance of finding work in that field. Would I be prepared to do any kind of work, he wanted to know. A facetious answer formed itself inside my head but thankfully didn't see daylight and instead I mumbled a humble 'of course.' He gave me the usual lecture about staying out of trouble, having the rest of my life to think about, not too late to make a new start, etc., etc. He made an appointment for me to see him the following week.

Money was now a serious problem. Paying for the hostel, clothes and food had eaten up nearly everything, including the £200 from Julia. It wasn't difficult to see how so many ex-cons rapidly found themselves back inside. The attitude was, if I do some thieving what have I got to lose? I might get away with it and if I don't, at least back in prison I'll have a roof over my head and food on my plate. Back in the early 1970s I had been in Marlborough Street Magistrates' Court doing some research. Two men had come before the magistrate on a charge of being drunk and disorderly. They pleaded guilty and told the magistrate that if they were fined they had no intention of paying the fine so he should send them to prison. They were fined fifty pence each. These indigent men knew where they would be better off. Well I wasn't at that stage yet and I wasn't happy at the thought of stealing but hunger is a wonderful motivator. At the supermarket I selected a loaf, some butter and a couple of apples. By the time I got to the till I was sweating. I'd never stolen anything in my life and here I was with a packet of ham and a chocolate bar stuffed into my pockets. Thankfully the checkout operator was more interested in talking to her neighbour than taking any notice of the uncomfortable-looking man in front of her. It seems that Janice 'didn't know you could catch it like that'. I would love to have known what Janice caught and how, but on this occasion I thought that discretion was the better part of not being nicked so hurried on my way. When I got back to the hostel and unloaded my ill-gotten gains I felt ashamed. So it's come to this, I thought. How easy it would

be to become emboldened by this small success and become
more and more brazen in my attempts to avoid destitution.

The following day saw me at the Job Centre. Outside were little
huddles of men smoking. The Job Centre had a no smoking rule
and the pavement outside was littered with stubs. I wondered
what these men were up to. I later learnt that unscrupulous
employers hire unemployed people to work on the black. They
get paid at a lower rate but since they pay no tax or national
insurance and are also getting their benefits they are happy to do
the work. The employers are happy too since they are paying
low wages and avoiding paying employer's contributions. All of
this was unknown to me at the time. I went inside. A notice told
me to wait until I was called. After ten minutes or so a besuited
young woman came out and called me in. And so the endless
form filling began. When we got to the point of understanding
why I was unemployed it surprised her little that I was newly
released from prison. No doubt she had many such clients. I
could not help getting a little frisson of amusement when I told
her what I had been in for. There was little discussion about
finding me a job. No doubt she thought me unplaceable. I was
told I would be sent a giro in a rather unspecific few days. But
where to send it? I told her it should be sent to the hostel,
although I had no idea whether I would still be there. And as it
turned out I wouldn't, though where I did end up I find almost
incredible, even now.

An empty afternoon brought thoughts back once more to finding
Alice. I had the address in Aylsham but would that yield any
more success than Holloway? Being down to my last few pounds
I decided that I would try and get away without buying a ticket.
In fact I had no choice. Enquiring at Victoria I learnt that I was
already at the right station for Aylsham. I also took care to ask
the fare. There was no difficulty in boarding the train, no barriers
or ticket inspectors. I settled back to watch the world unfold
before me. Ever since I had been released I had the feeling of
seeing everything for the first time. I would not have believed it
was possible to forget so much. We were well into the journey;

we had just stopped at Faversham and I was beginning to hope that I might be able to get away with my ticketless journey without any hassle. I heard the guard coming through the carriage and decided that the humble, innocent approach would be best. I made a pretence of searching through my pockets, while the guard stood there patiently, the expression on his face conveying his frank disbelief in my charade.

'I seem to have lost it.'

'Where are you going?'

'Aylsham. I had it a minute ago. Maybe I dropped it when I went to the toilet.'

'Did you buy a single or a return?'

'A return.'

'So how much did you pay?' I told him the price I had been quoted. He had clearly come across this ruse before.

'You'll have to buy another ticket.'

'I understand that but I haven't got any money.'

'You'll have to give me your name and address.' This seemed a pointless exercise as I could tell him anything and he had no means of checking. I did so.

'Arnold Salmond.' My mind almost went blank, unable to think of a single road name until I remembered Chase Way. 'Ninety-eight Chase Way, Southgate.' I hoped there wasn't a ninety-eight.

The look of incredulity on his face hadn't changed. I sensed that this wasn't end of my problems so far as this journey was concerned. I checked out the wall map and saw that the station before my stop was Adisham. I resolved to get off there, avoiding a possible welcoming committee at Aylsham. At Adisham I leapt off the train and scuttled out through station exit. I needn't have bothered. No-one pursued me or tried to collect my ticket. I now had to find my way to Aylsham. I hoped it wasn't far. A taxi was parked outside the station, the driver leaning against the bonnet smoking.

'I'm trying to get to Aylsham. Is it far?'

'Jump in.'

'Sorry, I've got no money. I'm going to walk. I just want to know how far it is.'

'It's about a mile. Turn right out of the station, keep following the main road.'

I hadn't gone more than a couple of hundred yards when the taxi drew up alongside me.

'Jump in.'

'I told you, I'm skint.'

'So you'll have to have a free ride then.' I got in.

'This is very good of you.' My statement implied a question.

'I was booked to pick someone up from Adisham off the train before yours but they didn't turn up. I thought I'd wait and see if they were on the next train but all that turned up was Mr.Skint. Anyway where are you going?' I gave him the address.

As we drove into the village I was struck by how similar all the houses were.

'This looks like one big council estate.' I remarked.

'That's because it was pretty much all built at the same time, in the twenties.'

'What, you mean there was nothing here before?'

'Pretty much. It was built for the coal miners.'

'Yeah, I heard there were mines down here, but that sounds odd to me. When I think of mines I think of the north or Wales.'

'Comes as a surprise to a lot of people.'

'So where was this mine?'

'Snowdon's the nearest to here but there were several. Betteshanger only closed last year. That was the last one.'

'I get the feeling that you might have had something to do with it.'

'Yep, twenty years down the pit, and now I'm driving this old banger around, picking up people with no money.' We both laughed.

Coniston Drive consisted of a mixture of semi-detached, detached and terraced houses; too modern to have been part of the original development of the village. Number forty-two was a semi. It was fronted by a rather unkempt garden and had an out of control creeper climbing up the front wall. I thanked the taxi driver, who sped off in search of fatter prey. Buoyed by my pleasant reception in Tenterden Road, I was perhaps unprepared for the rather hostile face of the woman who peered out of the door.

'Mrs Baker?'

'Yes. We're not buying anything.'

'It's alright I'm not selling anything. I'm trying to track down some old friends who lived in the Tenterden Road house before you. I wondered if they had given you a forwarding address.'

'That was ages ago and anyway as far as I remember they didn't. They said they would get the post to sort that out.'

'You mean redirection?'

'I dunno. Is that what it's called?'

'Do you remember where they were moving to, what part of the country?'

'No, I don't know anything about that.' This said as the door was being closed inch by inch. One last attempt. I might at least get a surname. I had no idea whether it had been Alice selling the house or whether she had at that time been married.

'Can you remember the name? Was it Travis or was it some other name?'

'I thought you said they were your friends.'

'Yes but I don't know whether my friend had married, in which case she would have had a different name.'

'I don't know anything. My husband dealt with everything. What are you after anyway? Are you really a friend? Maybe I should call the police.'

The last thing I needed. I thanked her and left. So a complete dead loss. Was that it then? End of the trail? Back on the train to Victoria I reflected on these few days since my release. Had I done better or worse than an ex-con murderer might expect? I had been lucky to find the hostel and Jean's friend Sam at the clothes shop. My meeting with Julia had been a disappointment but much more than that it was a shock, to see what she had become, how ill and near death she was. My dealings with officialdom were neither good nor bad. My search to find Alice had not been a success. As I sat there with these thoughts, watching the pleasant English countryside pass by, I heard a familiar voice. It was the same guard who had been on the outward train.

'Hello there, managed to find your ticket?'

'Not as yet,' was my somewhat feeble reply.

'I'm not really surprised. Victoria hadn't sold anyone a return to Aylsham this morning. And that address you gave doesn't exist. It's been checked. So you'll either have to buy a ticket or leave the train at the next stop, or perhaps you'd like to tell your story to the railway police when we arrive.'

Subterfuge had run its course. 'OK, I'll be completely honest with you. I've just been released from prison. I've got no money and after tonight I will be homeless. I can give you my name but that's all I can give you.'

Almost before I had finished speaking a voice came from behind.

'I'll pay his fare.' The guard and I both turned to see a tall, elegant women holding out a ten pound note. She was dressed in a black suit and a white blouse. Her dark brown hair was tied back and a pair of glasses were poised half way down her nose. The guard took the money and gave me the ticket. He gave me a nudge. 'Looks like you've cracked it mate.' And then laughed. The irony was not lost on me. The dishevelled pauper and the smart businesswoman. Hardly a match. I looked back. The woman had her head bowed, seemingly reading something. She seemed to have no further interest in me but I had to thank her. I went and sat beside her.

'That was very kind of you.'

'Not at all. I couldn't concentrate on my reading while you two were having your contretemps.' With this she turned back to her papers. Evidently I was dismissed. I resumed my seat. Was that an act of kindness disguised as self-interest, or was she as ruthless as she sounded? I was soon to find out. Walking up the platform at Victoria she caught me up.

'Are you really going to be homeless after tonight?'

'Apparently so. Why?'

'You can stay with me. I've written the address down. Can you get there before ten tomorrow? I have to go out then.'

I'd hardly mumbled a yes before she was off. Then she stopped, turned, and came back.

'I don't know your name.'

'It's Jim, Jim Mallinson.'

'Oh,' she paused, then 'oh yes.' She looked at me intently and then she was off again, long strides taking her quickly out of sight. What was that all about? What did she mean by 'oh yes'? I looked at the piece of paper she had given me. Colette Montague-Brown, 17 Balmoral Mansions, Ennismore Gardens, SW7.

13

Back at the hostel I sought out Jean and told her my news. She got out an A to Z and we tracked down the street.

'That's a very posh area. Who is this woman?'

'I've no idea.'

'You want to be careful. She might just fancy a bit of rough then sling you out on your ear. There are posh women like that.'

'Well, I've got very little to lose. I'm going to be homeless from tomorrow anyway. There supposed to be sending my Giro here. Will you hang on to it for me?'

'Of course, call in any time. I'm always interested to see how my boys are getting on.'

With that I went up to my room to spend a hungry evening, excited by the thought of what tomorrow might bring.

In the morning I was up, washed and dressed and breakfasted before eight o'clock. I was anxious about the ten o'clock deadline. I said goodbye to Jean and set off. It took me very little time to walk the couple of miles to Knightsbridge and I was at the mansions before nine o'clock. Now I was anxious that I had arrived too early. Maybe she wouldn't be up yet. I didn't want to get off on the wrong foot. I hung about outside for a few minutes. The building looked extremely posh. It was six storeys high, very much in an art-deco style. A set of wide steps led up to the main entrance doors, through the windows of which I noticed a man peering at me. I finally gathered my resolve and went in. The man, who I could now see was uniformed, and who I took to be some sort of porter, looked at me as though I was something to be scraped off the bottom of his shoe.

'Yes?' was his amiable greeting.

'I've come to see Mrs Montague-Brown.'

'One moment.' He made a call and then, 'will you go up? You need the fourth floor, number seventeen.'

I needn't have worried about being too early. Colette was dressed and clearly ready for work. She looked down at the two carrier bags I was holding. 'Is that it?'

I confirmed that that indeed was it. 'Put those down for a minute I'll show you round.'

The hallway itself was almost as big as some people's living rooms, and the living room itself, which we entered through a door on the right was as large as some people's whole apartments. Opposite the door was a fireplace surmounted by a huge gilded mirror. Either side were bookshelves right up to the ceiling. Two sofas were arranged in an L, one facing the fireplace, the other at right angles. In the window overlooking the street was a small table with two chairs. It was loaded down with books and papers. In the corner between the window and the wall was a television. On the wall opposite the fireplace were two more bookshelves and between them a single painting of a country scene. Double doors took us through to the dining room, smaller than the living room but to my eyes still enormous. In the centre of the room was a large table surrounded by six chairs and on which sat a candelabra. On the right hand side was a sideboard on which there was a large amount of silver. The window at the back of the room overlooked a courtyard where there were a number of garages.

A single door on the left took us into the kitchen. There was a table and chairs here and I imagined that this was where most eating was done. A door on the left took us back into the hallway. There were three doors leading off to the right. Colette stopped in front of the first one.

'This is your room. I've put out the bedding but haven't made the bed. I'm sure you can manage to do that yourself.'

I felt overwhelmed by all this. I had never been anywhere like this and found it difficult to understand why I was being welcomed into such a place. I needed to say something.

'Look, before we go any further I think you should know something about me.'

Before I could go on she came back with, 'you're a convicted murderer. Is that what you wanted to tell me?'

'Well, yes, but how did you know?'

'My uncle defended you, Edward Molyneaux. He always believed you were innocent.'

So that was why she had hesitated at the station. She had recognised my name.

'He never said so.'

'He wouldn't. That wouldn't be the professional thing to do. We defend according to the instructions of our client. Our belief in innocence and guilt doesn't come into it. That's the jury's job.'

'So you're a barrister too. Is Mr Molyneaux still working?'

'Oh yes. He's a QC now. I often see him at the Bailey. I'll give him your regards, shall I?'

Before I could reply she went on. 'Here's a door key. You won't need one for the main door. The porters are on duty 24 hours. The door's locked at night but they'll let you in. I'll mention to Trevor - that's the one you saw - that you are staying for a bit and he'll tell the others.'

She gave me the key, then fished in her hand bag and pulled out a fistful of notes. 'Get yourself some decent clothes. I don't want people to think I've taken in a tramp.' She laughed.

'There's plenty of food in the fridge and in the cupboards. Just help yourself. I get someone from Harrods to stock me up every week. Anything special you want just leave them a note.'

With that she was out of the door. I walked into the living room and sat down. I found it difficult to take in this change in my circumstances. I looked down at the hand that was still clutching the pile of notes. There were all tens. I counted them; there were twenty-four. There was a great deal I wanted to ask Colette but principally why was she doing this? What did she expect from me? I wandered round the flat, opening drawers, poking in cupboards, looking at everything. The books in the sitting room were mostly law books, though there was a fairly substantial couple of shelves of light fiction. I didn't notice any cookery books and when I looked in the fridge I think I understood why. It was full of food from Harrods, Fortnum and Mason, Marks and Spencer, nearly all of which needed little preparation. This was what I was to help myself to. The silver on the sideboard was solid, not plate, and the cutlery too was solid silver. A nice haul. I suddenly remembered that Colette hadn't shown me the bathroom. I rather timidly pushed open the door adjacent to mine. It was the right one. It was a bare place, just soap and a couple of towels. There were none of the kinds of things I would normally associate with female occupancy.

I thought I should heed the instruction to get myself some clothes. I took the lift down and as I walked past the desk insouciantly called out a 'good morning Trevor.' The reply of 'good morning sir, my name's Philip; Trevor will be on duty this evening' and the accompanying look I got put me firmly back at the bottom rung. As has so often been said, no group of people has a better-defined sense of rank and status than those in subservient roles.

I thought I would give Sam some more business and I needed to pay for the jacket he had given me. Behind the counter was a new face; a dark haired, dark eyed young woman in jeans and a shirt, intently reading a celebrity magazine. As I walked past her she didn't even look up. I wondered if the shop had been sold but everything looked much as before and then the mystery was solved as Sam, looking more unkempt and sweaty than ever popped out from behind a rack of clothes. He came and shook my hand.

'I thought you'd sold the business.' I nodded towards the counter.

'Annette. She comes in and helps out now and then. Anyway what can I do for you?'

'I want to buy some more stuff and no, I don't need the bargain rail this time.'

'Good, I never make any money off that.'

I chose more trousers, shirts and a pile of underwear and took it to the counter. Annette managed to tear herself away from the magazine and started to tot up my purchases.

'You've also got to take for this jacket. I can't remember how much it was. Sam'll tell you.'

'It's alright you can have it.'

'Come on Sam, that's not right. You'll bankrupt yourself. I want to pay for it.'

'Yes, giving away my inheritance!' This from Annette.

'Oh, is this your daughter Sam?'

'Niece. I haven't got any children. Three nieces, my two sisters' children. Can't wait to get their hands on my money.'

Annette laughed and I took this to be part of normal family banter. I thought how nice it would be to be included in that banter. Before I went to prison family hadn't meant a great deal to me. My parents I took for granted, as all young people do, and I had never been very close to Steve. I wondered where he was now. Still in the same house in Walthamstow or had the aspiring Therèse persuaded him to find something bigger, more in keeping with their elevated status? I was making a lot of assumptions of course; that Steve had continued to make upward progress in his career; that he was still with Therèse. Their children would be grown up now and almost certainly would not remember me. I could not imagine them as adults. Finding Steve, if ever I decided to look for him, could turn out to be as difficult as finding Alice.

I had spent the afternoon rediscovering central London. By the time I returned to the flat I was tired and hungry. I was still not as fit as I would like to have been. I started to think that my muscles must have atrophied during all those years in prison. I delved into the fridge and fished out a prawn, smoked haddock and cheese bake. It sounded wonderful but I had to find out how to cook it. It advised using a microwave. I had never used one before. In fact before that day I had never even seen one. I found it hard to believe that something could be cooked in two minutes but there it was, steaming and smelling wonderful. I had just skewered the first forkful when the front door opened and I immediately felt guilty, as though I was stealing the food. Quite irrational of course. Colette came through to the kitchen.

'That smells good. Is there any more?'

I went to the fridge once more and found another. 'Yes, shall I microwave it for you?'

She agreed that I should and asked me to get out a bottle of Chablis that was in the fridge. I assumed that I was to share the wine and took down two glasses. So there we sat, a companionable couple, sharing a bottle of fine wine.

Tongue loosened by the wine I said, 'there you are Colette, I've cooked my first meal for you.'

She laughed, thank goodness. I then wondered should I be using her first name.

'Is it OK to call you Colette. I didn't mean to presume.' She agreed that it was.

Always anxious to fill a lull in conversation I asked, 'Were you in court today?'

She nodded. 'How did it go?'

'Terrible. Some little idiot who thought it was OK to beat up his girlfriend because she wouldn't do as he asked.'

'Oh, do you mean something sexual?'

'Precisely, and something disgusting.'

'I take it you don't get to choose who to defend.'

'In theory you might, but if you kept refusing briefs you'd soon be out of work. Anyway, I'm going to take a bath. Thank you for cooking for me.' She smiled.

The fact that she didn't use the bathroom near my room answered the question. She obviously had her own bathroom. I felt that we were off to a good start. That she had sat down and eaten with me and laughed at my little joke seemed encouraging. I just hoped that I wouldn't once again prove to be a complete idiot as I had done so often in the past. To have fallen on my feet in this way seemed nothing short of miraculous. How long this good fortune would last I didn't know but if it only lasted a week than it would have been much more than I could have ever hoped for.

14

In the next few days I took to exploring London, visiting galleries and museums, even going to the cinema on a couple of occasions. Colette came and went according to no fixed schedule. When our paths crossed she always exchanged a few words with me but altogether I did not see much of her. She often retreated to her room for the evening to watch the television there. It was after about a week or so that things took a turn. A turn for the better or the worse I could not say, but definitely a turn. I was settling down to watch a football match when I heard a voice behind me say, 'time to pay the rent.' I stood up and turned to see Colette standing in the doorway, completely naked. She had the most wonderful body. I guessed she was four or five years older than me but you would not have thought so. She was tall and slender and beautifully proportioned. I followed her to her room.

I had imagined that Colette might want to play a dominant role in love making, matching the strong, forceful person that she seemed to me to be but in fact she behaved in quite the opposite way. She was very gentle and submissive and seemed to prefer cuddling and little gestures of tenderness. We lay together after, like spoons in a drawer. She seemed in no hurry to get up.

'That was very nice Jim. I suppose you were completely starved in prison.'

I didn't feel like telling her about Julia. 'Slight understatement,' was my response.

'Was there any hanky, panky going on?'

I laughed but I knew what she meant. 'Yes but they all tended to end up together. We decent criminals wold have nothing to do with them.'

She laughed in turn. I went on: 'what's your interest?'

'I see a lot of people who eventually end up in prison, although I do my best to keep them out, of course. But I've no idea what life there is really like.'

'You couldn't possibly imagine it. It's not just the conditions inside, it's the awful grinding endlessness of it. It rots you. And because you can't imagine it, neither can you imagine what it's like for me living here with you. I could never have dreamed...' I just trailed off, leaving the sentence unfinished. Emotion had got the better of me. She turned and kissed me.

'Colette, changing the subject for a minute, otherwise I'll be blabbing. I notice you're wearing a wedding ring but I don't see any signs of a husband.'

'Oh Geoffrey, don't worry you'll never see him. He never comes here.'

'So where does he live?'

'At our house in the country. If ever he comes up to London he stays at his club.'

'You've got a house in the country as well as this?'

'Yes, I go down most weekends. In fact I'm going down this weekend.'

'What does Geoffrey do?'

'Nothing. At least he has no gainful employment. He trained as a civil engineer but gave up after a few years. This is the trouble with inherited wealth. He spends his time with his dogs and his guns on the estate, monarch of all he can shoot.'

'So why do you work?'

'I would go mad down there with all that country set – bloody horses and dogs and county shows and all that crap. I enjoy my work and I think I'm doing something worthwhile.'

Which later got me thinking about my own situation. The probation office and the Job Centre were somewhat surprised when I gave them my new address, but asked nothing further. They had probably written me off as an unemployable dead loss. I suppose I would have liked to work at something useful but it was difficult to see who would employ a convicted murderer. There were, no doubt, employers who would employ me to do some menial, soul-destroying job for next to nothing but I wasn't about to seek them out, particularly given my present lifestyle. I had been so much enjoying this new life of luxury and indolence that I had hardly given a thought to my search for Alice. But like a questing tongue with a hollow tooth, inevitably I came back to the subject. I didn't know which was the stronger emotion, the desire for revenge or the need for some kind of justice, or maybe they were the same thing, and I had no idea what form either might take. The problem was that I seemed to have reached a dead end. If only I knew which part of the country she was in. Maybe she had emigrated or died. How do you find someone? I knew there were private investigators who did this kind of thing but I assumed they would be expensive and anyway I didn't want to make that kind of fuss. I was far happier acting on my own. The fewer people who knew what I was up to the better. I decided I would have one last attempt.

It occurred to me that the only way I could get hold of Alice's forwarding address would be through the Post Office. Clearly they weren't going to give it to me just like that. I wondered if the postmen might have access to the information I needed. In order for redirection to take place the new addresses had to be known to the postmen sorting the mail. Might one of them remember it, or at least know which part of the country it was in? I decided it was worth a try. The following morning I made my way back to Tenterden Road. I didn't want to be found loitering again so I started walking the length of the road quite briskly, turned round at the end and came back. Perhaps even this behaviour would be regarded as suspicious, or possibly that of a madman. The trouble was that I had no idea when the post was delivered but there was a small general store at the far end of the road. Perhaps they would know when the post came. As I entered, a bell clanged with a loudness to wake the dead. A woman wearing a sari appeared from the back room.

'Can you tell me what time the post usually comes?'

She looked at me blankly. It was not a question she was expecting to hear. I tried again and then we were saved by the appearance of a man, also from the back.

'What do you want?' I was starting to get paranoid. Why was everybody so suspicious of me?

'I'm trying to catch the postman. Do you know what time he comes past?'

He looked at his watch. 'Usually about now. Why, what you want him for?'

I muttered something I hoped they didn't hear, thanked them and left. After another half hour of brisk walking the postman appeared. I walked up to him and then alongside as he delivered his letters.

'I wonder if you can help me. I'm trying to get in touch with the people who lived at No.33. Do you happen to know where they've moved to? Did they have a forwarding address?'

'No idea mate.'

He was young and I guessed hadn't been doing this walk very long. Of course I had no idea when Alice had moved. It could have been years ago.

'If they had redirection you'd have that information at the sorting office, wouldn't you?'

'Possibly, but we wouldn't be allowed to give it to you?'

'Do you know where the information would be kept?'

He didn't answer. He was young, more likely to be short of money than an older person. This was the moment.

'Well if you could get hold of it for me it would be worth a hundred quid to me.'

'Why's it so important to you?' He hadn't said no.

'It's an old friend. I knew she was going to move and she told me she would send me her new address. I was in Africa at the time – voluntary work - but the letter never got there. I've tried everything and you're my last chance.' I knew that giving someone a 'good' reason to break the law would work a lot better than the contrary. 'So what do you think?'

'I'll see what I can do. A hundred quid you say?'

'Yes, so shall I see you here tomorrow?'

'No, leave it till Monday'

I agreed that I would and thanked him. There was just one problem. I didn't have a hundred pounds. Back at the flat I hoped Colette wouldn't be late. I was very nervous about asking her for more money. She came in at about six o'clock and went straight to her room. I heard the bath running. By the time she finally appeared in the kitchen I was a bag of nerves, which she could see straight away.

'Oh God, Jim what have you done? You haven't been shoplifting, have you, or is it something worse?'

'No nothing like that. I hate to ask you but I wondered if you could lend me some money.' The use of the word 'lend' was ridiculous, as we both knew.

'Oh is that all. For God's sake stop hovering and pour us a drink.' I did as I was bidden.

'I'm going to give you my bank card. You can withdraw what you need. I'll get on to the bank to give me a second card next week.'

'But what about you, won't you need it?'

'I've got some cash and I've got my credit card. In any case I won't need any money this weekend. As I told you I'm off to be bored in the country. I expect I'll spend most of the time sleeping. You'll need the code. It's easy to remember. It's the year Churchill was born – 1874. And you're thinking why did I choose that. One of my husband's distant relatives was secretary to Churchill. It's how I make the link if I forget.'

Once again I was impressed by Colette's extraordinary generosity. I mumbled my thanks.

'Don't go on about it. As I told you, I'm not short and your best way of thanking me is to stay out of trouble and confirm my faith in you.'

And therein lay the problem. Getting hold of Alice's address might well lead to just the opposite result. But before I could do anything else I had a weekend to kill. Where could I go? What should I do? It was June and not the weather for staying indoors. I found a map of London on the bookshelves. Despite the fact that I was a Londoner and had spent the first twenty-five years of my life living there, there were vast tracts which were completely unknown to me. Cricklewood, Hounslow, Dulwich, Rickmansworth, Sydenham, and on and on. What were these places? What went on there? My eyes lighted on Walthamstow, one place I did know; the town where my brother Steve lived. What was he like now? Was he even still there? I could remember the house, though not the address and I doubted the phone number would be the same even if I could remember it. It seemed inevitable that I should at least try to contact him. A rejection would leave me no worse off than I was currently. I would sleep on it and decide what to do in the morning.
I felt very shaky using Colette's card, imagining some screaming alarm would go off when I put in the code. I had written it down for fear of forgetting, something, apparently not advised. It seemed like a miracle when money came out. Such machines had not existed in 1975. I took the Victoria line to Walthamstow Central and changed there on to a train going to Wood Street. It was just a couple of minutes to Steve's house, if it was still his house. I felt the familiar nervousness coming over me again. I kept telling myself that I had nothing to lose but of course I was lying. I would lose a great deal to be spurned by the only family I had. Greenway Road was a street of houses that looked as though they should be semis but in fact they were all joined together in a terrace. They were fronted by a large bay which stretched across the front of the house. It struck me as a curious design. All the houses were the same. And there it was, number

twenty-two. Now that I was there I remembered the number. A large Mercedes was parked at the front. I walked past, and then back again, peering in through the front window. I couldn't see anybody but somebody must be in, otherwise why would the car be there? I walked back to the corner of the street and stood for a few minutes. I took a few deep breaths and resolved to knock come what may. I reached the house but before I could knock a young woman came out. She looked at me, her brows knitted in suspicion.

'Are you looking for someone?' I was surely looking at one of my nieces. It was either Briony or Jessica. I felt my eyes filling with tears. Her look changed to one of anxiety. 'Are you alright?'

I seemed to have lost the power of speech but finally whispered, 'are you Briony?'

'Yes but who are you?

'I'm your uncle Jim.' And then I started crying properly.

She put her hand to her mouth, 'Oh my God!' She went back to the door and shouted for her father. I stood by the garden gate trying to recover myself. Steve appeared.

'What's all the panic?'

'It's Uncle Jim.'

Steve came slowly down the path, 'Jim?' And then recognising me threw his arms round me. 'I'm so sorry. I let you down. I'm so sorry.' Soon we were both crying.

'It's alright Steve. You had your family. I understand.'

We said nothing for a few moments, still hugging each other, and then I said, 'Is this legal?'

We both laughed and the tension was broken.

By now Thérèse and Jessica were at the front door. I looked up at them. The look on Thérèse's face was one of anxiety. Anxiety out of concern for me or anxiety at what problems I might be bringing her family, I could not say, until she took my face in her hands and kissed me. Without anyone saying so, somehow we all drifted inside, Steve gripping my arm.

'What about some coffee?' this was Thérèse. There was a general affirmation. Steve's living room spoke of his elevated status in life. Leather furniture, an expensive stereo system in one corner with a stack of CDs, a huge television in the other. On the mantelpiece were sculptures in what I took to be bronze. There were paintings on two of the walls. We all sat down and now the questions began. Steve wanted to know how long I'd been out, where I was living, was I working, how had it been, and so on. The girls were clearly fascinated to have a convicted murderer in their house and couldn't stop staring.

As the coffee arrived now it was my turn. 'I had no idea if you'd still be here.'

'We've thought of moving somewhere larger a number of times but the girls like it here. It's where they grew up; their friends are all around here; we're near the forest and the station. It's very convenient.

'And how's work?'

'Oh, you know, boring but profitable.' Steve was an accountant.

'You girls not thinking of following in your dad's footsteps?'

Briony got in first, 'you must be joking, adding up numbers all day, like a living death.'

Jessica was not slow in echoing her sister's sentiments.

'There you are Jim, the youth of today, ignorant as the day is long. We have machines, computers if you like that do all the adding, as you call it. Accountancy is a little more complicated than you imagine.'

Thérèse joined in, 'you don't mind your dad's money though do you, every time you want some new clothes or a CD, or want to go to one of those awful rock concerts.'

Steve came back, 'completely spoilt the pair of them.'

All of this was being said in a light-hearted way and I felt the wonderful warmth of it. This was a close and loving family and I longed to be part of it.

I changed the subject, 'so what are you girls doing?'

'I'm at Sussex doing my first year of law and Jess is in her second year of A levels.'

'What made you choose law?'
There was no immediate reply and Briony looked across to her father, who it was who replied, 'it was partly because of you. The girls didn't really remember you but I told them later on that they had an uncle and they wanted to know all about you, why they hadn't seen you. I had to tell them about your conviction. When Briony knew that you had been wrongfully convicted she became fascinated by the whole subject of the law and decided that's what she wanted to do.'
Briony looked at me,' Uncle Jim can I ask you something?' I nodded.
'You didn't do it, did you?'
'No, not that one, but I did all the others.'
There was a pause, and then relieved laughter.
Jessica joined in, 'what was prison like?'
'It was horrible. Don't let anyone tell you any different. You may hear stories about colour televisions and prisoners leading a life of pleasure while other people work to pay for them. Forget it. It wouldn't matter how pleasant life in prison might be, the real punishment is the loss of freedom. Just think about all the things you are going to do this weekend, things that you choose to do, that you take for granted. Imagine that all taken away. Not having the warmth and love of your mum and dad.'
Jessica had started to cry.
'I'm sorry. I've gone on. I didn't mean to.'
'Don't apologise Jim. It's good that the girls know these things. Talking of mums and dads, a thought has just occurred to me. Would you like to see mum and dad's grave? It's in Chingford cemetery. We could go now, if you like.'
I was taken aback. I hadn't thought about my parents for years. I had blocked them out of my memory and I guessed that must have been through the guilt that I felt; that I had made their last years so miserable, maybe even hastened their deaths. It was agreed that we would go. The girls wanted to come to. The drive there brought back memories as we passed familiar landmarks; the waterworks, so intriguing to a child behind its high wooden

fence, the town hall, and then our old school. Less happy memories for me there, though Steve had done well.

'Why were you such a swot Steve?'

'I guess I wanted to please mum and dad, particularly mum. It meant a lot to her that we had got into the grammar school.'

'How easily we take them for granted, and then they are gone and there is no more chance to say all that we might have said. Do you think they believed in my innocence?'

'They certainly wanted to but they found it hard to believe that the police and the courts could get it wrong.'

'That's it. They were simple, hard-working, honest people, and because they were honest themselves, found it difficult not to believe everything they were told. I remember dad's funeral. You came and sat with me. Everyone ignored me except Auntie Jane. Didn't she used to live round here somewhere, Ulverston Road?'

'We've passed it.'

'What happened to her?'

'She died a few years ago. She always thought you were innocent, told mum so. It's dad side of the family that were sceptical. They were always were a bit snooty.'

We had reached the cemetery. It was a long walk to the grave. It was overgrown. A broken vase leaned against the headstone.

IRENE MARGARET MALLINSON

BORN 8TH JUNE 1920 DIED 2ND FEBRUARY 1978

GEORGE ALBERT MALLINSON

BORN 16TH OCTOBER 1919 DIED 11 MARCH 1980

'Steve they were no age at all. Now I feel even worse. They didn't even live long enough to get their pensions.'

'Yes but you were innocent. It wasn't your fault.'

'It was in a way. If I hadn't been so intent on playing a trick on that woman, a nasty trick, I would never have got myself into such a mess, with all that followed. That's the part I feel guilty about.'

The drive back to Steve's house was silent. We were greeted by Thérèse at the front door. 'You'll stay for lunch Jim?'

'I don't want to put you to any trouble.'

'It's only soup and sandwiches, so no trouble at all.'

I accepted. I was enjoying being part of this family. Over lunch the girls wanted to know about prison life. By hints and winks they let me know that they wanted to know what happened about sex.

'Well, you'll have to work it out for yourself.' Steve and Thérèse were looking appropriately embarrassed but the girls hadn't finished with the subject and Briony asked the obvious question, although in a nicely obtuse way.

'Do any of the men go – you know?'

'Yes a few do go – you know, and that's the end of that subject.' Steve and Thérèse looked relieved.

But the girls weren't finished with prison. It was Jessica's turn. 'What do you do all day? Can you read?'

'Oh yes, there were very good libraries in both the prisons I was in, but you have to remember that a lot of these men are scarcely literate and have very little interest in books.'

'Well, why's that?'

'Many of them have had very poor home lives. Absent fathers, chaotic mothers, parents with alcohol problems. A lot of them truanted, which was how they would get into trouble in the first place, shoplifting and the like. A lot of their homes would not have had a single book in them. I wonder if you realise how lucky you are, to have a secure home with parents who love and care for you, praise and encourage you when you do well. Many of these men never had anything remotely resembling what you have. I would give anything to be part of a family like this.'

I had got a little bit carried away with myself and there was an awkward silence. Finally, Thérèse got up and came across to me. She put her arms around me saying, 'Jim you will always be part of this family.'

I found myself blabbing again. 'Thérèse that's the kindest thing that anyone has said to me in fourteen years. Means so much.'
Thérèse was in tears too and the girls joined in. Even Steve found it necessary to fish out a handkerchief.
On the train home I thought about the day's experiences. Experiences that were exponentially better than I could have imagined but experiences that puzzled me too. This family, my brother's family, who had ignored me for the best part of ten years, had now, apparently, taken me to their bosom. Thérèse was the most surprising. She had always regarded me, I thought, as Steve's ne'er do well little brother and that ending up in prison would have been no surprise to her. Maybe I had misjudged her, mistaking her hauteur for dislike. In any case, none of the past mattered now. I was in no doubt that the words said and the emotions expressed were genuine and it was a wonderful comfort to me – I was part of a family.
For fourteen years, time had stopped still, during a time when I, like Steve, might have met and set up home with someone, had children, had a career. I wondered if it was now too late to meet someone, to have that kind of relationship. I day-dreamed for a while, thinking how that might be but then told myself not to be so stupid. How would I support this family? I had no job and was never likely to have one, or at least one that would give me a decent standard of living. The quest for Alice lurked for ever at the back of my mind and these thoughts brought it once more to the front. I had just to wait until Monday and with any luck I would finally have her address.
Sunday was a long day. I could not settle to anything. I wandered round the flat. I took books off the bookshelf and put them back again. I turned on the television and turned it off again. I thought if I went to bed earlier, the morning would come quicker. It didn't work. I couldn't sleep at all. I lay there most of the night, leaping ahead in my mind to the confrontation, how it would play out, the words I would say, the regret she would express. I woke with a start to find I had overslept. I put on my clothes, skipped breakfast, skipped washing and set off for Tenterden

Road. I was in a panic that I might I have missed him. I was there at about the same time I had seen him on Friday but might he have come earlier? There was nothing I could do but wait but what was this? A woman was delivering the post. I went up to her as she came past and walked alongside.

'What's happened to the other chap?'

'You mean Rory.' She had a half smile on her face.

'Is that his name?'

'He broke his leg on Saturday, playing football.'

Before I could sink into a slough of despond she continued, 'he gave me something to pass on to you, if you're the right person.'

'I think I must be.'

'And you've got something for him, is that right?'

I agreed that I had and pulled out the notes. She took them and gave me a slip of paper: Mr and Mrs Dalby, 17 Saxon Road, Saxmundham IP17 1ED. So this was it, or I hoped so, the lack of first names caused a doubt. I thanked her. After a few paces I turned back.

'Where's Saxmundham?'

'It's in Suffolk.'

'Right, thanks, and thank Rory, hope he gets better soon.'

Back at Victoria I learnt that I needed to take a train from Liverpool Street station. I was impatient to go but I had to see my probation officer on Monday and I had an appointment at the Job Centre on Tuesday. It seemed that they might have 'something' for me. I dreaded to think what that something might be. If Sunday seemed interminably long, the wait until Tuesday was almost beyond endurance. On Monday I was happy to tell Mr Rawlings about my job prospects. He showed little interest. For him it was just a box to be ticked. On Tuesday I saw the same young woman, who told me she had arranged an interview for me the following week at a catering suppliers in Vauxhall. She wasn't too sure what the job entailed but it was manual work of some kind. The employer knew that I had been in prison but not what for. He was prepared to give me a chance it seems.

So here I was then on Tuesday afternoon at Liverpool Street Station about to board the 14.45 to Ipswich, excited but at the same time trepid. I boarded, found a seat, the whistle blew and we were off.

*

15

'What's up Alice? You look as though you've seen a ghost.'
This from Dalby.
'I…such a surprise. Hello Jim.'
She made no move towards me. No kiss, no hand shake, but she hadn't screamed for me to get out of the house. She hadn't told Dalby to get rid of me. It made me wonder how much he knew of her past. It was a good start.
'Can you stretch supper to the three of us   your curry banana of whatever it is?'
'Yes, yes. It's carbonara. Yes…I'll…' She didn't finish the sentence but hurried back to the kitchen. Dalby stared after her.
'Well you've really given her a surprise. Never seen her so shaken up.'
'It's been a long time. Perhaps I should have written first.'
'Anyway now you're here we should celebrate. I've got some rather nice Médoc. I'll get a bottle.'
He went out to the kitchen. I expected to hear raised voices but there was nothing. No communication at all. This was all to the good. I had expected an immediate rejection, a threat to call the police, which is what I had been prepared for. Dalby returned with the wine.
'Where are you staying?'
'I'm not sure. I suppose there's a hotel somewhere.'

'You can stay with us. We've got a spare room. Two spare rooms actually, although one is full of junk.'
'Well, I don't want to put you to any trouble.' The stock response.
'Not at all. It'll be good for Alice to have some company. We haven't really made many friends since we came here.'
Dalby opened the wine and almost completely emptied the bottle into three glasses. Alice returned with the food. She had given herself a tiny portion which she barely touched. Her wine though disappeared rapidly. Dalby, seeing her empty glass, went to get another bottle. Alice looked at me but said nothing. I smiled at her. Her colour had returned but in an unhealthy looking way. Her throat was flushed and she had bright red spots on her cheeks just beneath her eyes. Dalby returned with the second bottle and replenished the glasses. Now came the question I'd been dreading.
'So Jim, what have you been doing all these years?'
'Nothing very exciting. Trying to teach English to young Italians who weren't interested in learning.'
Alice said nothing. I hoped Dalby was the kind of person who was more interested in talking about himself than about others. I wasn't to be disappointed.
'So Adrian, I take it you work down in Ipswich. What do you do?'
He poured himself some more wine. I prepared for a monologue and Alice started to clear the plates.
Dalby chimed up, 'I've invited Jim to stay. The spare room's OK isn't it?'
'The bed's not made up. There's a lot of stuff in there. I really don't think…' She trailed off.
'You don't mind being amongst a bit of clutter, do you Jim?' Dalby was not about to lose his audience. Once I agreed I didn't, Alice left. Soon after, there was a lot of angry banging coming from the kitchen.
'I've actually got two businesses. I run an insurance agency, got a couple of girls who take care of most of the paperwork. The

agency's in Tacket Street, good position, right in the town centre. Doing well. My other business is a bit of a launch into the dark, or at least it was, it's OK now but caused a few anxious moments. I used to have hair before I started on that.' He laughed.

'There was a redundant mill near the town centre by the river. I thought it might be convertible into apartments. People, young people especially, seem to like these industrial buildings turned into flats. I bought the mill and got an architect to work up some plans, just outline, to get a feel from the council. They weren't opposed and then we got down to the detailed planning. I'd completely underestimated the work involved. Just the planning stage took three years. There were problems with the builders. The first one walked off the site. Anyway we eventually got it done and we advertised the flats. I called it the Dalby Apartment Store. Seemed to catch on. We let every one within a few weeks. The rents are good. Lot of young professional people who can afford them. Mind you I won't see a penny for ten years. Had to take out a huge loan secured against the building. If I default the bank gets it.'

While Dalby talked I kept prodding him with nods and little approving sounds. Dalby was a safe subject. I didn't want it turning to me. By now we were on to a bottle of malt and Alice had gone to bed. Dalby continued for some time. He clearly thought that he was a pretty good businessman and liked to let me know. I didn't mind. I rather liked him. He was warm and friendly. I didn't see him and Alice as a couple, at all. Having now met him, my first impression when I had seen him walking home was confirmed. They were a decidedly odd couple. I would love to have known how they met but was wary into digging too far in case the digging was reciprocated. Dalby caught me nodding. I apologised, telling him I'd missed out on sleep recently. He showed me to my room, the room now made ready by Alice, and I gratefully went to bed. I lay awake for a little while, anticipating once again the sound of raised voices, but heard nothing. The morning beckoned.

I got up to find that Dalby had gone. The two little girls were sitting at the breakfast table, one eating toast, the other cornflakes.

'I don't know your names.'

'I'm Rosie and she's Tess', this from the elder one.

'Do you suppose this toast and coffee is for me?'

'Yes, mummy said so.'

I helped myself. Alice returned from the kitchen without acknowledging my presence.

'You girls finish your breakfast and go and clean your teeth.'

When they were gone she finally turned to me. 'When I get back from taking the girls to school I went you gone. If you're still here, I will call the police.'

'Didn't Adrian tell you, he invited me to stay for another night?'

'I don't care, I want you gone. Why have you come here?'

Before I could answer the girls returned. Alice gathered their things and ushered them out of the door, banging it with considerable force. It was a good question. Why had I come here? What was going to happen next? Dalby's warm reception had changed things somewhat. He and Alice were not on the same side, not working from the same script. It strengthened my hand. But to do what? The door banged again.

'Right, I'm calling the police.'

'Are sure you want all that fuss? What would the neighbours think?'

'I don't care what the fucking neighbours think. I want you out of that door and out of my life.'

'Maybe you should have thought about that more carefully before you framed me for a murder you committed.'

'You framed yourself, leaving your fingerprints all over the place.'

'Yes I did, but stupidity isn't murder.'

'You didn't answer my question before. Why have you come here?'

I noticed that she hadn't approached the phone. 'I'm not sure, but I had to come. I had to find you, to confront you. There needs to be a resolution.'

I had stood up. I noticed that Alice's mood had changed from belligerence to apprehension.

'Take your clothes off.'

'What! That's it then. You're going to rape me. That's your resolution, is it?'

'Do as I say.' I made a step towards her.

She started to undress, carefully folding her clothes and laying them on a chair. Finally she was naked. She stood, her shoulders slightly hunched, her hands vaguely covering her nakedness, her eyes cast down. It was a pose of submissiveness. In a few short minutes she had gone from aggression to capitulation. I looked at her. She was still beautiful, her body hardly changed after fourteen years and two children. Despite myself I felt pity for her. Now it was I who capitulated. I suddenly felt that I needed to go no further. The mission was at an end.

'Get dressed.'

'What?'

'Put your clothes on.'

I turned and sat down again. Behind me I heard no movement. She was still standing there. I poured myself some more coffee. I felt a hand on my shoulder.

'Jim, aren't you going to have sex with me?'

'No, get dressed. I'm going to leave you in peace now. It's finished'

'But I want you to. Jim, I want you to fuck me.'

The use of that word caused me a frisson of arousal. But it was a trap. I could see that.

'I get it. We have sex and then you cry rape and see me locked up for the rest of my life. You always were sly.'

She walked away. She was doing something at the other side of the room. She came back and put a piece of paper in front of me.

It read: *I have asked Jim Mallinson to have sex with me. I write this of my own free will.* She had dated and signed it. Her closeness, the smell of her, so familiar, found me weakening.
'Why Alice?'
'I just want you.'
'A few minutes ago you wanted me out of the house, now you want to have sex with me.'
'I can't explain.'
Was I going to regret this? She led me to the bedroom. It was as good as it had ever been. It was as though we each had memorised for all those years what pleased the other, just for this moment. I lay there afterwards, cuddling this woman who I hated. Everything that had happened to me after leaving prison seemed extraordinary. It was difficult to come to terms with it all. Was life outside meant to be as extraordinary as this? Was it the contrast with the dull, unending routines of prison life that made it so?
'Are you going to phone the police then?'
'Don't be stupid. It wasn't a trap. You should know something. Adrian and I haven't had sex for five years.'
'How come?'
'After Tess was born I became badly depressed. I couldn't function at all. I was taking anti-depressants. I lost all interest in sex. To tell you the truth, it didn't make a lot of difference. Adrian isn't a highly sexed man and he wasn't very good at it either. I was nearly always left hanging, having to finish myself off. He's a kind, gentle man but you need something more than that in bed.'
'Hang on a minute. If you haven't been having sex, presumably you aren't taking any precautions.'
She laughed.' Don't worry, it's the wrong time of the month.'
'Thank goodness for that. Alice I'm going to have a shower and then I'm going. I'm going to leave you in peace. You won't see me again. Something strange has happened here. You cannot believe the vengeful thoughts I've had towards you over the years; the things I'd fantasised about doing to you. Longing for

the moment I could get to you. I still don't understand why you did what you did but I don't care anymore.'
'No Jim, don't go. Please stay. Adrian wants you to stay.'
'What's the point?'
'I can't explain. It's something else I can't explain. Please stay.'
I eventually conceded that I would but first I needed to get some fresh air, to try and get my head organised, to make sense of everything. I agreed that I would be back for lunch. Stepping through the door, Saxmundham seemed like a different place. Everything I looked at smiled benignly back at me. People too, no doubt because of the big grin on my face. Had it really come to an end, this fourteen year quest? Might it not raise its ugly head again in some unguarded moment? I wondered if Angela at the church was free. There was no-one in the church so I tried the vicarage. Angela looked pleased to see me again and invited me in. She immediately noticed a change in my demeanour.
'I think you bring good news.'
'I'm not sure. That's why I wanted to talk to you. I found the person I told you about, still full of vengeful thoughts. I seemed to have him where I wanted him. Then all of a sudden it didn't matter anymore, and I don't know why. I felt enormously relieved. You remember your comment about all ye who are heavy laden? Well you were right. I was heavy laden and now that load has been lifted from me and I feel wonderful but I'm struggling to understand it. Do you think I've found God?'
It wasn't a serious question and she laughed, 'I'm pleased for you Jim. I don't think that doing something awful to whoever it was would ever make you feel better. In avoiding doing whatever you were going to do you have in a way been magnanimous, if only by default. I think that's why you feel the way you do. You have found that you are bigger than the problem that was troubling you.'
'I guess you're right. Well, thanks once again. It's been good to talk to you.'
'Jim before you go I'd like to say a little prayer with you.'
'But I ...'

'I know you're not religious but would you just do this for me?' I agreed that I would. Her prayer was along the lines of thanking the Lord for helping me to find the right path and lifting the burden from my heart. I didn't mind. It was a small thing to do for someone who had been kind and understanding. She finished with a 'God bless you Jim.' I put my arms round her and kissed her cheek. She didn't seem to mind.

Alice had prepared a salad for lunch. As we ate it she kept looking across at me and smiling. It was unsettling. What was she thinking? What was she planning? Despite the nature of this renewed acquaintance I was still wary of her. I was wondering if I had made a mistake in agreeing to stay. Impulsiveness had been my downfall. I didn't want it to be so again. Perhaps my first instinct to leave had been the right one. I was soon to find out what all the looks and smiling had been about. After lunch, Alice left all the plates on the table and disappeared to the bedroom. She called me. It wasn't entirely a surprise to find her lying naked on the bed. I went across and sat beside her. She put her arms round my neck. This gesture needed no interpretation and we made love once more.

I woke to hear a clattering sound from the kitchen. I looked at the time. I had been asleep for several hours. I got dressed in a panic, imagining Dalby coming through the door any minute. When he did so, it was with his usual bonhomie. The girls made a fuss of him, as I imagine they did every time he came home, then he and I settled into the living room while Alice fed the children. The malt was produced again and he poured us both an aperitif. Answering his question about what kind of day I had had produced a need for creative imagination. But in truth he wasn't particularly interested, happy to get the subject back to himself. At dinner the Médoc flowed once again into all our glasses and once again Dalby played the genial host regaling us with stories from his business. I wondered if the difference in Alice's behaviour and general demeanour was as obvious to him as it was to me. She had a bright colour and constant smile and laughed at everything.

Dalby had suggested that I travel down to Ipswich with him. Apparently he didn't normally work on Saturdays but he had some things to sort out at the office. At Ipswich I would catch the London train and he would go off to work. I hadn't really intended to set off that early but he seemed rather insistent and I didn't want to offend him so I agreed. In the morning Dalby seemed in a rush and I barely had time to say goodbye to Alice. I took her hand and kissed her on the cheek.

'So goodbye then,' was all I managed to say. Her eyes were filling up as she responded with her own goodbye, then quickly turned away.

We left the house far too early for the train we were to catch. At the station he guided me to a bench at the far end of the platform.

'You've realised by now that I wanted to have a word with you. I know what went on yesterday.'

Before I could say anything he went on.

'And I'm glad. Alice may have told you that for us things in that department have not been very good for a long time. It doesn't matter to me very much but I know that it matters to Alice. All I care about is her happiness and of course the children's too. You saw how she was last night. I haven't seen her like that in years. So I'm going to ask you something, as a favour really. Will you came and see us again, soon?'

I was lost for words. This man who I had cuckolded was asking me to do so again. I had liked Dalby from the outset but for this I admired him. It seemed that there was nothing he would not do for the happiness of his family. I think I mumbled a vague affirmative before he went on again.

'Look, don't commit to anything now. Just bear in mind what I've said. You've got the phone number.'

We boarded the train and sat in silence. Dalby turned to me now and again, smiling. I had no words. At Ipswich we got down and he pointed out the platform for my London train. He took my hand in both of his with a final admonition not to forget what he had said. Approaching Colchester once more on the London train it seemed improbable that it had only been four days since

I last passed this way. What was less improbable was that I was no longer that same man who had made the outward journey. I went over in my mind everything that happened since I stepped off the train in Saxmundham. Not one part of it seemed normal, ordinary, everyday. Maybe that was because for so long I had been unused to the ordinary, but I think not. When I set out on this journey I could not have imagined how it might conclude, how I would achieve peace of mind. True to say, of course, that I had spent very little time imagining anything at all. I had merely had my 'mission'.

In my mind I went over once again that scene with Alice. How I told her to undress, her compliance, and my complete inability to know what to do next. I don't really know why I had told her to do that. Was it to prove that I had some kind of power over her? In truth I was in a very weak position. She had only to call the police and it would have been all over for me. So another question is, why had she complied? Was she in some way accepting her guilt, her malign part in all this? A bigger question still was what had happened to me in that moment. Did I see the futility of what I was set upon or was her submission to me all that I needed to salve the wound? I had no answers. All I knew was that I was happy to be relieved of the awful burden of revenge.

If that scene was extraordinary enough, what followed was no less. I might dismiss her demand for sex as nothing more than the lust of a sexually frustrated woman, or on the other hand was it part of her capitulation? Again I had no answer. The third extraordinary element of this encounter was Dalby's request that I continue to see his wife; that I continue to cuckold him. So strange to me was all of this, that I can imagine that if these things had been written in a novel they would have been condemned as being completely unrealistic; the fantasies of a schoolboy. One more question remained, would I accept Dalby's request to visit them again? In that moment I thought that I probably would but there was no need to make any decision yet. Time was needed to digest all of this and nagging away at the back of my mind was a tiny little doubt, did I really trust Alice? I regretted that after our love making I hadn't asked her why she had shopped me all those years ago. We had been, so I thought, in a loving relationship. Perhaps I had been deluding myself. Perhaps I was just being used as a convenience until something better came along. Had that 'something better' been Dalby? Had he and his money been around at that time? Had Alice seen the chance to kill two birds with one stone – to get rid of me in favour of Dalby and at the same time make sure someone other than she was convicted for her crime? Another regret was that I hadn't found out how those two had met, how long they had been together so all of this was speculation. And now I was back at Liverpool Street Station. I made my way back to the flat hoping that Colette would be there. I felt a need for company and someone to talk to. She had left a note to stay that she hoped I had enjoyed my trip and that she was off to the country once more.

16

Saturday morning I got up and mooched around the flat, unable to settle to anything. These last few days had unsettled me. I felt the need to talk to someone, to get the perspective of someone else. Of course, in the days before prison, before we completely lost contact, it would have been Dave. For all the larking about we used to do Dave was a canny bloke. At school we all despised the system; said we didn't believe in working just to pass meaningless exams. We were rebels, refused to wear the proper uniform, took delight in being as scruffy as possible. What I hadn't realised was that I was the only one in our group who had actually put all of this into practice. The others certainly maintained their shabby exteriors and insouciant attitude towards study but at the same time were quietly beavering away in order to pass said despised exams. So they all went on to sixth form and university while I dropped out, an apparent academic failure. Dave had got a job in a brokering firm and the last I had heard was doing very well. In prison we had vaguely heard about the Big Bang in stockbroking of the mid-1980s, and how young traders were making indecent amounts of money sitting in front of a computer screen. I imagined Dave would have been among them. Where was he now, I couldn't help wondering. Getting in touch with Steve had given me a great deal of confidence but was it sufficient to try to contact Dave? After all, he hadn't given up on me. It was I who had sent him away. I felt that he just hadn't been able to cope with the prison situation.

Dave had lived in a small house in Chingford. If he had been as successful as I thought he must have been, it was very unlikely that he would still be there. All I could do was head there and try to get a clue where he might be now. It was a long walk from the station to Friday Hill. Number 27 looked much as I remembered it. Unlike so many others it hadn't been extended either upwards or sideways. Possibly the door was a different colour to the one I had last seen but it was too long ago to remember. Parked outside was a grey Peugeot with two child seats in the back. No way was that Dave's car. He regarded cars as a statement about their owners. Dave was definitely not a grey Peugeot. My ringing of the bell was shortly answered by a small boy who, before I could say anything, told me that 'we don't want any today thank you'. A man loomed up the hallway.

'Who is it Jonathan?' He came to the door.

'Hello, I'm trying to contact my friend Dave who used to live here. I wondered if you had any idea where he might have moved to. I'm assuming you bought the house from him of course. I'm sorry to bother you if that's not the case.'

'Are we talking about Mr. Frobisher?'

'Yes that's it, Dave Frobisher.'

'I did have an address for him. Epping way. It's a while ago now.'

'How long has he been gone?'

'Best part of ten years since we moved here. Come in a minute. I'll see if I can track down that address.'

I was taken through to a living room where a little girl, older than the boy, was arranging her dolls. She decided to tell me their names, conventional for the most part, with the exception of 'Tracey Checkout'. Clearly a child with imagination. The little boy was anxious to show me his lorries but before he could do so, the man returned.

'Here it is 7, Green Trees, Epping.'

It wasn't easy to get to Epping. A bus took me to Loughton underground station and from there I took the train to Epping. The railway here went on to Ongar. The first and probably only time I had been to Epping previously was with dad and Steve, way back in the 1950s. We had gone there to collect blackberries. How fascinating for a small child to see that the train to Ongar was pulled by a steam locomotive. Yes, steam on the underground – hard to believe. Green Trees was just five minutes from the station. It was a cul-de-sac of very large, detached houses. Number 7 had a Mercedes and an Alfa Romeo parked outside. Yes, Dave had indeed done well if these markers were anything to go by. I stood for a while looking in the windows, wondering if I might gain a glimpse of him. Finally, with considerable unease, I rang the bell.

The woman who answered the door looked haggard. Her hair had been inexpertly dyed a beige colour. Some of the roots had been missed. She had dark circles under her eyes and lines of worry on her forehead. Seeing me she touched her hair in almost involuntary movement but otherwise her demeanour was not a welcoming one.

'Hello. I'm an old friend of Dave. I was given this address. I hope I've got it right. Dave Frobisher.'

She hesitated then called back into the house. She twitched a nervous smile at me and then turned as Dave came up the hallway; a Dave I scarcely recognised. He was enormously fat, his great belly overhanging the waist of a pair of sports trousers. His unshaved face was flushed, and greasy strands of hair lay across his forehead.

'I don't believe it. Jim? For God's sake.'

He stepped out and caught me in a bearhug, his beard rasping against my face, and his alcohol breath filling my nose. 'You old bastard, you old bastard. When did you get out?'

Without waiting for an answer he drew me inside the house, ignoring the woman. As we passed I turned to her, 'I'm Jim.'

'Sorry mate. This is my wife Debbie. You remember luv, I told you about Jim.'

We went through to the living room, huge with leather sofas along two walls, a massive television in one corner and in the opposite corner an antique display cabinet full of small silverware 'This deserves a drink. What'll you have Jim – whisky, brandy, wine, beer.'

'Bit early for me, Dave.' It was a quarter past eleven. 'Any chance of a coffee?'

Debbie disappeared to the kitchen and Dave started plying me with questions. When had I got out? Where was I living? Had I got a job? Had I got any money? After that he apologised for not coming to see me, although I pointed out that it was I who had asked him not to come anymore. After this torrent it was my turn.

'When did you get married?'

'Ten years ago. Best thing I ever did.'

'No children then.' There were no signs anywhere.

'Oh yes, Tammy's seven and Nigel's nine. They're up at Debbie's parents for the weekend, up in Braintree. They love it up there. They've got a smallholding, loads of animals.'

Debbie arrived with the coffee. 'You'll stay to lunch Jim. There's plenty, isn't there Debs?'

She agreed that there was. Dave heaved himself over to a drinks cupboard, which was the lower part of the display cabinet and pulled out a bottle of brandy. He poured a good measure into his coffee. I declined his offer of the same.

'You still with the same firm?'

'Yes, senior partner now. Got a team that does all the work while I sit and read the FT.' He laughed. 'Not exactly like that, but quite a cushy number. Been some very good years. Both the kids are in private school, got a villa in Spain. You've seen the motors. Debbie's parents' smallholding, we paid for that.'

What could I say? He really had done well but I was shocked at the state of him. We spent the time before lunch reminiscing about school days, and our time after, as 'lads' out on the town. And as I sat there it seemed to me that we no longer had anything in common, except these distant memories. He had moved on, become a family man, done well for himself, matured into a middle age. For me, on the other hand, time had stood still. In terms of the development of my life I was still in my mid-twenties. Only the body had aged.

Dave insisted that we should have 'something special' with our lunch. I little doubted that this 'something special' would be alcohol of some kind, and that Dave had something of the same nature every lunchtime, even if less special. He took me out into the garden.

'Had this put in. Cost me a fortune but you can't keep good wine in a garage.'

He took me down a short flight of steps to a metal door which took us into a cellar under the lawn. The cellar was about eight feet wide and twelve or so feet long. The walls were concrete and the roof was held up by steel beams, which I had to duck under. There were bottles of wine from floor to ceiling. The bottles were arranged in bins, each bearing a label indicating the year and provenance. Dave took me to the far end. He pulled out a dusty bottle.

'Look at this. Petrus 1985 – two hundred quid a bottle, but worth it. I've got a really good wine merchant who gets me all the best years.'

I didn't like to say that I failed to see how a bottle of anything could be worth paying that price but I could see that Dave had moved into that category of person who had so much money that they had to look for silly things to spend it on. With a second bottle in Dave's hands we headed back indoors. Lunch turned out to be a chicken casserole. It was very good. While I was drinking my single glass Dave managed to finish the bottle and start on the second. By the time we came to the apple pie he was slurring his words and embarking on the kind of maudlin sentimentality which is the special reserve of the profoundly drunk.

'Best mate ever. Had brilliant times, didn't we? Felt terrible when you went to prison. Really upset me. I was angry too. Started slipping up at work. Thank God I met Debbie. She put me right, didn't you darling? Gave me two lovely kids. My beautiful kids.'

Debbie and I were exchanging glances. I felt embarrassed for her. No mystery now about her care-worn appearance. She had been a beautiful woman and could be again too but I could see that she had been driven down by Dave's illness, for that's what it was. She started clearing away the dishes and Dave and I went through to the living room. He fished out the brandy again and poured us both a large measure. I sipped at mine while Dave finished his and poured himself another. In no more than ten minutes he was asleep. I went out to the kitchen, where Debbie was loading the dishwasher. Before I could say anything, she spoke: 'bit of a shock for you.'

'How long's he been like that?'

'He's getting worse and worse but it started after what they call the Big Bang. They were all making so much money and he and group of others used to go for a drink after work. Over the weeks one drink became several, and then a hard core of them would stay until closing time. It was every night Monday to Friday. Weekends were not so bad until he got into his fine wines, had that cellar built. He usually has his first drink about ten o'clock. Says it's a pick-me-up to start the day.'

'I was worried that he might have started because of me being sent to prison. I know he was terribly upset.'

'Yes he was upset but it was a long time after that that he started.'

'What about the children. How do they cope?'

'They hate it when he gets all sloppy sentimental but otherwise they just ignore it. They seem to have adapted to it. He's a very good father, very loving. He never shouts at them, or me. He's not an aggressive drunk. Such a pity to see him become like this. I worry that he will kill himself if he goes on like this much more.'

'Has he tried to do anything about it – Alcoholics Anonymous that kind of thing?'

'Wouldn't hear of it. Couldn't cope with the shame.'

'Anyway, this seems a good time to push off.'
'Oh no, don't go. He'll be upset. He'll think you're disgusted with him. Come and look at my garden.'
We went outside. Beyond the lawn which covered the cellar was a magnificent flower garden. Seemingly arranged haphazardly, there were flowers of all shapes, sizes, and colours, not one of which I could identify. A curved path led to a little, hedge-enclosed arbour, where there was a stone seat.
'This is where I meditate.'
'Did you do all this yourself?'
'The flowers, yes.'
'It's wonderful. How often do you meditate?'
'I try to manage twice a day for twenty minutes or so, but it's difficult when the children are around.'
'Does it help?'
Before Debbie could answer Dave appeared. He looked terrible. His shirt had come out of his trousers and his flies were undone. Strands of dishevelled hair had fallen across his greasy forehead and spittle had encrusted the corners of his mouth.
'Just been admiring the garden, Dave. Done wonders.'
'Yes, very good.' He belched as he spoke.
'Dave, I'm going now. Been great to see you.'
'You too mate. Come again, soon.'
All the life had gone out of him. I had expected he would say more but he seemed happy for me to go. Perhaps he wanted to get back to his sleep. I noticed the moistness in Debbie's eyes but I don't think Dave did. I thanked them both once again and took my leave.

17

I spent a very unsettled Sunday, made worse by thinking about what I had seen out at Epping. Dave had everything I thought I wanted. He was where I thought I should have been at this stage of my life. More and more the thought of children occupied my mind. I felt that children must give a feeling of completeness, of being part of something, of a continuity. But what was Dave's story? Why the drink, the self-destruction? I had known Dave better than anybody, except perhaps my own family. I knew his parents. They seemed completely normal to me. He had no brothers or sisters, although there had been a younger brother who had died as an infant. Was there something there, some hidden mystery coming back to haunt Dave? While I was mulling all this over Colette returned. I was glad to see her.

'Ah Jim, just the man I wanted to see.'

'Really, why's that?'

'I've had the shittest weekend you can imagine.' I laughed.

'It's not funny. Stuck with a load of boring, blood sports morons braying on about how it's their right to kill small animals. Can you imagine?'

'No-one with a brain cell to spare then.'

'None. The women just as bad. Waffling on about who's getting married, who's getting divorced, who's doing what with whom. Pathetic.'

'Do none of them work?'

'One or two pretend they do. Probably spend half an hour a week in a charity shop and then have to have a lie down to recover.'
I laughed again and Colette joined in.
'Anyway what about you, how was your trip?'
I most certainly didn't want to give Colette any details about Saxmundham.
'It was fine, but I had a rather disturbing day yesterday.'
'Tell you what Jim, why don't you tell me about it in bed. Get a bottle and a couple of glasses. I need a drink and I wouldn't mind a therapeutic shag, either.'
'Happy to oblige madame.'
We drank and commiserated with each other; I for her awful country friends and she for my unsettling encounter with Dave.
'Colette, I've been meaning to ask you something.'
'Oh God this isn't a proposal of marriage, is it?
'No. Well not yet, at least. I'll have to get rid of that husband of yours first. And talking of murderers, do you remember the case of the female barrister who married a convicted murderer, got struck off, or whatever you call it. It was back in the early sixties.'
'Every barrister knows about Naomi Blaithwaite. Anyway, what about it?'
'Well I was just wondering about you and me being shacked up together. Might that harm your standing if it got known?'
'We live in different times and in any case Naomi was married to her murderer. You are merely a lodger.'
Mellowed by drink, enervated by our difficult days, we fell asleep in each other's arms, the therapeutic shag forgotten about.

Tuesday was the day of my job interview. I had been sent to the prosaically-named Catering Supplies Ltd of Vauxhall, which had a vacancy for a warehouseman. It wasn't far, so I decided to walk. The exterior of the company's premises was far from prepossessing. It had the appearance of a double fronted shop, the upper windows painted cream, the lower black. To the right hand side was a black-painted door, doing its best to divest itself of its paint. On the left of the windows was a vehicle entry, which was open. I guessed that no-one used the door so I walked in by the entry. In front of me was a series of loading platforms and beyond that I could see aisles of shelving stretching back a considerable distance. To my right was a row of three offices. In the first I saw two women sitting at typewriters; the second was empty and unlit, and in the third was a lone man, speaking on the phone. This I concluded was Mr Thompson, the man I had come to see. I wasn't sure of the protocol. Did I go straight to the boss or should I call in at the office with the two women? I chose the latter. I knocked and entered.

'Hello. I've come for an interview.'

'Mr Mallinson, is it?' and before waiting for a reply: 'just knock on Mr Thompson's door and wait.'

I did so and Thompson waved me in while still speaking on the phone and motioned me to take a seat. His call was quickly finished.

'Now then, Mr Mallinson.' He looked at some papers on his desk. 'Oh yes. What did they tell you about the job at the labour exchange?'

I suppressed a smile. Why was it people so long hung on to outdated labels?

'Not a lot really, just that it was a warehouseman's job.'

'Ok, well as the name of the company suggest we supply the catering trade – restaurants, hotels, cafes, firms cafeterias, government departments, anywhere food is involved. We supply everything except the food. Your job will be to unload lorries coming in with goods and load the vans going out on deliveries. We also have some small clients who come to collect their stuff themselves. With them it's a question of picking orders from the warehouse. How does that sound to you?'

'It sounds fine.'

Thompson stared at me for a while before going on: 'no point in asking what you've been doing up to now. Your probation officer says you were a model prisoner, which is good. What were you in prison for, if you don't mind me asking?'

'Murder.'

After a long pause. 'May I ask who you murdered?'

'I don't expect you to believe me, but I didn't murder anyone. I was framed.'

'So how does that make you feel?'

'As you would imagine. But I've got to move on, reconstruct what's left of my life.'

Another pause. 'So are you interested in the job.'

I agreed that I was.

'Is there anything you want to say to me?'

'I'm not sure what you want. Do you want me to beg you to give me a job?'

'No, no.' he looked flustered. 'Look, the job's yours, if you want it. Can you start Monday?'

We went through a few things; hours, pay, notice, other paperwork. Then it was all over and I walked out into the sunshine. I felt pleased, although I wasn't entirely sure why. A career in humping stuff around wasn't exactly what I had in mind for myself but I knew it was better to be occupied than moping around at the flat.

The following Monday Thompson caught sight of me as I walked into the warehouse. I think he had been looking out for me. It wasn't yet nine o'clock and he took me into his office.

'The boys don't turn up until the last minute. I didn't want you wandering around the warehouse like a lost sheep. When they get here I'll get Josh to show you the ropes.'

We spent an uncomfortable few minutes of inept conversation before, to our relief, Josh came very slowly through the entry; jeans half way down to his knees, untied shoe laces and hair arrayed in spikes and curls. He looked like a homeless person who had wandered in looking for somewhere to sleep. I learnt later that Josh was a refugee from a country in Africa, the identity of which I never discovered, and was probably never meant to know. Thompson called him over and introduced me. By this time the other men had arrived and more introductions were made. Mickey looked about eighteen. He was slight and moved with jerky movements, almost as though he was performing some kind of dance routine. He was always friendly to me and to everybody else, as far as I could see. I liked him. Marc was in his twenties. He spoke little but sang most of the time, always the same song. Although I knew French to some extent, I could never make out a single word of his song. I eventually asked him about it. It seems the song was in Auvergnat. His mother sang it when he was a child, which is how he learnt it. But he told me he didn't understand it any more than I did. His mother was one of the last people to speak the dialect but as far as he knew none of his generation did. It was a nice song nevertheless. The last of the group was Kurt. I guessed he was about thirty. He barely acknowledged me. He had a downturned mouth and the appearance of having a perpetual snarl.

Josh was only in his early twenties but he was the perfect foreman. He never raised his voice and when he asked you to do something it was said almost as a suggestion and you had the feeling that you would be doing him a personal favour. Kurt clearly disliked Josh and it was plain to see that he felt that as the eldest he thought he should be in charge. He would have been a terrible foreman. He was a natural bully and would have put everyone's back up in no time at all. That first day Josh showed me the warehouse. There were five aisles, about thirty yards long, stacked from floor to ceiling. The first aisle contained crockery of every kind. The second was pots and pans and all kinds of cooking vessel. Who knew that there five different kinds of fish kettle? The third aisle was devoted to glassware, cutlery, and kitchen implements. The fourth aisle was for clothing, everything from toques to shoes. The fifth was devoted to table coverings, napkins, cleaning equipment and chemicals. It took surprisingly little time to get the hang of things, work out where everything was, and working life soon settled into a routine.

About a month after I'd started at the warehouse, just as I was leaving, Mr Thompson, who I now knew as Simon, came out of the office and called me back.

'Have you got a minute?' I nodded. 'Fancy a pint?'

I agreed that I did. We walked down to the Fentiman Arms. Simon ordered the drinks and we sat down in a corner.

'So how's it going? You settling in alright?'

'Yes fine, no problems.'

'Not overstraining your intellect?'

I laughed. Simon was well aware that I was vastly overqualified to be a warehouseman, and nearly twenty years older than most of the other men.

'I've had a letter from your probation officer.'

'I thought you might; checking up on me. Question one 'has he murdered any of your staff?' question two 'how many?''

For some reason Simon thought this was much funnier than I did and laughed so much it started me off. We had nearly finished our pints and drinking on an empty stomach had made us a bit tiddly. Trying to suppress our laughter made it worse and soon we like a pair of giggly schoolgirls. We were just recovering when I came out with: 'taking a bit of a risk leaving all those sharp knives lying around,' which started us off again. Simon got up to get another round.

'I'll get these', I said.

'You can't afford it on the money I pay you.'

'You're right, you miserable sod.' And we were off again. Simon got the drinks.

'You know, I liked you from the start.'

'Why was that? Was it my disinclination to grovel?'

'I guess that was part of it. It showed a strength of character that I thought might have been extinguished after everything you've been through.'

'Did you want me to grovel?'

'No it wasn't that. It was more that I expected it. We've had ex-cons here before and it's the usual form.'

'Why do you take them?'

'I try to do my bit. Not everyone has the best start in life and people deserve a second chance. That's what I feel anyway.'
'So what happens to them?'
'Unfortunately, so far, every one we've taken on gets caught stealing. It seems it's hard for thieves to break the habit.'
'So you won't put up with theft but you don't mind the odd murder.' Another fit of giggles ensued.
'Well that's the point, isn't it? Just because you're a murderer doesn't automatically mean that you will also do other sorts of crime. And before you say it, I know you didn't do it.'
We stayed for a third pint and talked about the business, how Simon had originally got involved with it. He told me about his family, his hopes for his two boys, both sports mad. He asked me little about myself, perhaps not wanting to intrude into what had been a negative experience. We shook hands on the doorstep of the pub and went our separate ways. I felt I had made another new friend in this strange new world of 'outside'.

18

In these early weeks at the warehouse I thought little about Saxmundham and my strange experience there. In fact the memory had taken on something of a dream like quality. However, I couldn't forget the invitation from Dalby and had to decide what to do. My thoughts about Alice were now completely different. The compulsion had gone. If I went to see her and Dalby it would be because I wanted to, not because I was being driven to. So I had a decision to make. If I did nothing, that in itself would be a decision, and I felt that I should make a positive decision; either to write a note and explain that I wouldn't be coming again, or phone and make arrangements to come. By the time my visit to Saxmundham was five weeks behind me I felt it was time to make that decision. Someone had once given me some advice about decision making. He said toss a coin and see how you feel about the result. Then you'll know what to do. Well that's what I did and the decision was to go to Saxmundham once more. That casually made decision was to have results far beyond anything I could have imagined.

So here I was once again, back on the train to Suffolk. I found it hard to think back to the state of mind I had had on that first journey, that awful compulsion. If today I had been told that I could not get to Saxmundham, perhaps because of a strike or an accident, I would not have been overly concerned. It really wasn't that important to me. And as that thought passed through my head it created a question: so why are you really going? I reviewed the possibilities. In the first place there was the fact that Dalby had asked me to come as a favour to him. Then there was the sex with Alice, which was good, no doubt about that. But was that enough? After all I hardly knew Dalby. I liked him but I could not count him as a friend, after just one brief visit. As for the sex, well to put it crudely, I had other options – Colette, although it's true to say it was always at her behest, which was not an entirely satisfactory situation. So was there something else? Was I perhaps attracted to the bizarreness of this situation? I knew now after all my years in prison that people are attracted to excitement. They want to see or participate in events that are out of the ordinary run of their lives. When all our other needs are satisfied we seek diversion. So was this it? There was another possibility. Was I still fascinated by Alice? Did she still have some kind of hold over me? After all, during my fourteen years in prison I could not stop thinking about her. Was that just the longing for revenge, or was there something else?

By the time the train slowed for the stop in Ipswich I had come to no clear conclusions, nor in reality could I. Dalby was on the platform waiting for me. We had agreed to travel together on the little train to Saxmundham. Dalby was his ebullient self. He was excited by a new venture. He had opened a second insurance office in Ipswich and was already drawing in new business. I couldn't help liking him. He was one of those people that is completely out front, nothing hidden, no nasty surprises. I think it is hard for people like that to understand that not everybody is like them; that there may be those with hidden motives and desires; people who are furtive and deceitful. Perhaps that was why the relationship with Alice worked; he could see no wrong in her. He did not know the woman I did.

The woman in question opened the front door with a big smile. She told us that she would see to the children and get on with dinner. Dalby took me to the living room and poured us both a large malt. Alice wasted no time putting the children to bed and then from the kitchen we heard singing.

'See the effect you have?'

I said nothing. It was still hard to believe that this man was content that I had come to his home to make love to his wife. The meal appeared; a roast with the usual accompaniments. Alice had gone to a lot of trouble, seemingly on my behalf. I was starting to feel uncomfortable, more so when I took notice of what Alice was wearing. It was a short red dress, buttoned at the front, the top three buttons undone. It was clear she was wearing nothing underneath. The food was eaten, the wine poured, the chatter continuous, mostly from Dalby. At one point as Alice reached across for some vegetables a breast fell out. She seemed in no hurry to put it back. She was more than a little drunk. Now Dalby looked embarrassed too. The way the chairs were arranged around the table meant that he couldn't see Alice as she went out to the kitchen, hoiking up her dress to show me her bare bottom. I hadn't visualised things like this. I thought everything would be very discreet. I was feeling claustrophobic, as though I'd wandered into a maze with no way out.

I was relieved when Alice went off to the kitchen and Dalby and I went back to our armchairs and more malt. The effect of the alcohol made it difficult to follow Dalby's plans for the future of his business. I smiled and nodded at what I thought were appropriate moments but eventually it became too difficult to any longer express interest and I excused myself and went to bed.

I was in my cell and they were trying it again. It was the same four. I struck out and shouted at them: 'get off you bastards.' I heard a voice calling my name. I got out of bed and stood confused. A light went on and there stood Alice, naked.

'Jim what's the matter?'

I sat down on the bed, my head in my hands, resetting my brain.

'Who were you shouting at?'

'I thought I was back in prison and they were trying it again.'

'Who was trying what?'

'About a year in, a gang of morons tried to bugger me.'

'What!'

'Yes, rape in prison is not that uncommon. Anyway these idiots thought that I was stuck up, needed taking down a peg or two. They came to my cell and tried to rape me. I fought like a maniac. I was quite badly hurt but they didn't succeed and they didn't try again. I'd managed to land a few blows and they probably thought it wasn't worth it. Did you touch me? What are you doing here anyway?'

'I tried to get in with you and you went berserk.'

'I thought we were going to wait until tomorrow when Adrian was out with the girls.'

'I know, I just couldn't wait.'

'Go back to bed. Adrian will miss you.'

She kissed me and left. I was more convinced than ever that this should be my last visit.

Next morning Alice was impatient for Dalby to leave with the girls. Again I felt embarrassed on his behalf. Alice was not behaving well. Once Dalby had left Alice started to steer me towards the bedroom. I stopped her.

'Alice I'm leaving.'

'What, you can't. Why?'

'I thought your behaviour last night was terrible. Didn't you see how embarrassed Adrian was?'

'Oh the boob thing. That was just an accident.'

'It wasn't just that. It was everything, the flashing for example.'

'But he didn't see.'

'No but I did and I didn't like it.'

'Jim I didn't take you for a puritan.'

'You're not getting it are you. It's your attitude to Adrian which is all wrong. Think about what he's doing for you; arranging for another man to come to his home to have sex with his wife. This man who works hard to provide for you and the children, who clearly adores you, and you're treating him with contempt. I don't want to be part of that.'

'I'm sorry Jim. I was overexcited and drunk and felt so randy. That won't happen again. Please can we make love?'

And we did, once in the morning and again in the afternoon. It was as good as ever.

The evening was quiet. Even Dalby for once wasn't his usual chatty self. I had intended to leave the next day but I could see Dalby was disappointed. He had wanted to show me his new office. I could hardly say no. I liked Dalby and this seemed little enough to do for him. We drove to Ipswich rather than taking the train. His new office was in Friars Street, not far from his other office. I could see a lot of money had been spent on this new venture. The whole shop front was glazed with frosted glass to waist level and clear above. Central double doors gave entry. Inside were three desks and chairs, all expensive Swedish-design. A row of filing cabinets sat on the back wall.

'Come and look at this. What do you think?'

Dalby showed me what I recognised as a computer, even though I had never seen one before.

'This is going to make all the difference. All the information about every client is going to be stored on here, their policies, their claims, it will tell me automatically when their renewals are due and print out the notices. That's the printer there.'

Although I couldn't know it then, I was one day going to be very familiar with the workings of that machine. It had been agreed that rather than return to Saxmundham I would take the train back to London there in Ipswich. Dalby saw me to the train with once again the suggestion that I might return soon. I said nothing but at that moment I thought a return visit anytime soon would be very unlikely. Once again Alice had shaken me up. What was it about her that was so unsettling?

Back at work things took an unusual turn. In our less busy moments, when there was no or little loading to do, Josh would ask us to go into the warehouse and tidy the shelves, make space for new deliveries. Kurt never took part in this. In fact he did as little work as possible. He would disappear off into a corner and read his newspaper. He sometimes read the same newspaper for several days in a row. On this occasion I caught sight of him moving his finger along the page and mouthing the words as he did so. It was clear that reading was a problem for him. I hesitated, aware that his attitude to almost any approach was one of aggression. But then I thought to myself, you're bigger than that, this bloke needs help. How to begin though?

'Hi Kurt. You know you can get help with that.'

'What?'

'Reading, literacy.'

He stood up. 'What you trying to say, killer?' He'd taken to calling me that after he found out about my murder conviction.

'I'm saying you can get help if reading and writing are a problem for you.'

'Listen killer, I don't need no fucking help from you or anyone, so fuck off and mind your own business.'

By now he was shouting and had attracted the attention of the others. Simon came out of the office. He wanted to know what all the shouting was about. We told him it was nothing, which he didn't believe of course, and we all dispersed. At the end of the day I called into his office.

'I guess you'd like to know what that was all about this afternoon. I didn't want to say anything in front of Kurt but I'd approached him about his reading problem. I thought I might be able to help. I had some experience when I was in prison. It's a sensitive subject but if you don't break through the barrier of admitting you need help you'll never get anywhere.'

'I thought there might be a problem there. I gave him some labels once to put on some boxes. They all ended up in the wrong place. I didn't ask him again. So what can you do?'

'Well nothing personally but there are literacy classes. Perhaps if you had a word with him. If he can't learn to read and write properly he'll still be doing this when he's sixty. Before you do that though, if you're willing, let me find out where the classes are.' Dave agreed.

There was an adult institute not far away, to which I went along one evening. I enquired about literacy classes and was taken along to see the tutor. She was perfect. She was a woman, I

would guess in her sixties, floral blouse and tweed skirt, hair in a bun and glasses dangling on a lanyard. She would present no threat to Kurt and his image of himself as a man. It was a small class and yes she would be happy to take on another student. That was the easy bit. The following week Dave spoke to Kurt. He made out that being able to read was likely to be more important in the future working in the warehouse and suggested the classes to him. Much to the surprise of both of us Kurt agreed to give it a try. The following Wednesday evening I met him outside the warehouse and we walked to the institute. He said nothing at all. By the time we had reached the classroom he was shaking. I felt so sorry for this man who so often could only express his feelings in anger. The tutor was as perfect as I thought she would be. She gave him a big smile, told him how lovely it was to see him, and led him by the arm to a desk. I felt considerably relieved and just hoped that he would stick at it. For the next few weeks whenever we encountered one another in the warehouse Kurt avoided all eye contact. I had no idea what that meant but after about four or five weeks I found out. One morning Kurt took me behind some boxes. He shoved a small package at me.
'What's this?'
'Chocolates, for you.'
'Why?'
'You know.'
'Thanks but that's quite unnecessary. So how's it going?'
'Alright. I've learnt more in these few weeks than in ten years at school.'
'Well, that's brilliant.'
'Just one thing. Don't say anything to the others. And killer,' a rare smile broke his face, 'thanks.'

19

The weekend after this incident I made my next trip to Saxmundham. Alice was on her best behaviour, dressed demurely at dinner, a little drunk but acting appropriately. There was no midnight visitation and she showed no impatience in waiting for Dalby to take the girls out once more. Once they had gone though she unleashed herself at me. She lost no time in undressing herself and then she was pulling at my clothes, grabbing me, being really quite aggressive. Once we were on the bed she really surprised me.

'Hit me.'

'What?'

'Hit me. Slap my face.'

'Alice what's going on?' I found these demands anything but erotic.

'I want you to hit me. It's what I deserve, everything I've done to you and to Adrian. Do it.'

I gave her a half-hearted slap to her face. He response was to slap me really hard and call me useless. That did it. I slapped her. She demanded that I hit her again and again. I started to find it arousing, although I wasn't sure why. Maybe I felt she was right, that she deserved to be knocked about. After a couple of minutes of this we were both panting hard.

'Now tell me what I am.'

'What?'

'Tell me I'm a whore, a slut, a bitch, all that kind of thing.'
I came out with a long stream of invective and then we were at it like maniacs. I think it was the best sex we'd ever had. When it was all over we lay there completely wasted. Alice cuddled up to me, stroking my chest and my face and telling me I was a sweetie. It made me a laugh, thinking about what I had just been doing to her.
I thought now would be a good time to find out a little more about Dalby.
'How did you and Adrian meet?'
'Why do you ask? Is it important?'
'Just curious. Is it a secret?'
'Not at all. He worked for the insurance company I dealt with.'
'What, and he just asked you out?'
'No, I saw him a couple of times in the office, several times actually, and we sort of got on and he asked me if I would like to go for a drink.'
'So what were you seeing him about that needed so many visits?'
'God, this is like a police interrogation. Why does it matter?'
Alice was clearly uncomfortable with these questions, which only intrigued me further.
'Well if it's a secret, I won't ask any more.'
'If you must know it was about the mortgage insurance policy.'
'You mean the pay-out you got after Laura's demise.' I hesitated to say murder. There was a silence while I thought about this.
'So you knew him at the same time you knew me.'
'Well obviously, but there was nothing more than going for a drink.'
Maybe not but it could have been that she was lining Adrian up for when she got rid of me. Maybe I was right in that getting me framed for the killing of Laura cleared the path for a new and more 'profitable' relationship. There were more questions that I wanted to ask but I decided to leave it for the moment.
'While we are interrogation mode. I want to ask you something.'
'Go on.'

'When you came to the house that first time and you made me undress, what were you going to do?'

'It's a good question but the answer is I had no idea. I had barely thought beyond that moment of confrontation. It was curious. I had thought so long about that moment, had endless fantasies about what I might do and yet just then seeing you standing there none of it mattered anymore. I suppose in some subconscious way I told myself that those fourteen years had gone, that there was nothing I could do to recover them so what was the point in doing anything to you? That wasn't a conscious thought, just hindsight, speculation. I cannot tell you how relieved I felt. I was determined just to leave and never see you again. But the evil temptress seduced me!'

And so life settled into a pattern. I would see Colette now and again but mostly we pursued our own lives. She seemed quite content that I should stay on in the flat, and that every so often we would make love. She knew nothing and asked nothing of my trips to Saxmundham, which now settled down to a once fortnightly routine. I looked forward to these trips. There was the company of Dalby, always entertaining in his own rather naïve way, and the sex with Alice, which got better and more inventive with every visit. On top of this, Saxmundham was a pleasant place. It was good to get away from the hum and thrust of London, and on fine days I had taken to walking in the country thereabouts. For an ex-con I seemed to be leading a dream life. I suppose the only lack I felt was the opportunity to have my own family, my own children. This lack was made ever more apparent to me whenever I saw the Rosie and Tess. I envied the affection they had for the parents, particularly for Dalby. They never questioned my presence at the house. To them I was just Uncle Jim.

It was near Christmas that I noticed a change in Dalby. He didn't meet me in Ipswich on that Friday, as he usually did. I carried on to Saxmundham and found him at home. He apologised saying that he had come home at lunchtime, feeling a bit under the weather. He didn't look well. His face had lost some of its usual ruddy glow and he had darkness under his eyes. He tried to cheer up over dinner but I could see it was forced. I wondered if he would still take the girls out, as he usually did on the Saturday of my visits, but he did so and things carried on as usual. Our love making on that occasion was subdued. I didn't feel right somehow to be making love to the wife of a sick man. Dalby was no better on my next visit two weeks later. I asked him if he'd been to a doctor. It seems he had but the doctor had given him no clear answers, suggesting that he might have a digestive problem, and he should perhaps ease up on the drinking. It was true that Dalby downed at least a bottle each night, often going well into a second. He was at that age – I had found out that he was fifty-two – when over-indulgence starts to catch up. I talked to Dalby and suggested that in the present circumstances my visits might be inappropriate. There was the problem of him always having to take the girls out, less easy on these cold and dark days. He told me that he didn't want to change anything. I had made Alice happy with my visits and he enjoyed my company too.

So we carried on. On the occasion of a visit in early February I was shocked to see how much Dalby had deteriorated. He looked ghastly and had hardly been to the office at all that week. The doctor was now taking things seriously and had ordered a number of blood and other tests. By my next visit these tests had given no clear indication of what was causing his problems. He was being frequently sick and had severe abdominal pain. His absences from the office were causing the business to suffer. It seemed to me that I might be able to help in some way and I put it to Dalby that if he could show me the ropes and be on call for advice I might be able to help out with the business. He did not reject the idea and in fact I had the impression that it was a rather like a life belt thrown to a drowning man. His first question was about my job. I had thought about this and I reckoned that Simon might let me go part time. When I returned to work on the Monday and asked him he chuckled. It seems that I had solved a problem for him. The owners of the company had been asking about staffing levels, implying that the business was overstaffed, so yes he would be happy for me to cut down to three days a week. I phoned Dalby to give him the news and he suggested that we meet that Thursday at the new office in Friars Street.

In my excitement about my 'new job' I hadn't thought about where I would be staying but Dalby insisted that I stay the extra two nights with him and Alice. At the office he told me that the most important part of the business was the renewals. These were indicated by the computer, which had now been programmed with all his clients' details. As each set of policies came up for renewal the notices needed to be printed off and sent out. When they were returned with the payments the women in both offices dealt with the financial side but the renewed policies had to be entered into the computer. This would be my job. The claims side of things was less important because in most cases clients reported directly to the insurer. In the case where they came to the office their claim was simply passed on to the insurer. The other major component that needed to be dealt with was new business. Dalby took me through the range of policies on offer. There were really only two major areas – household and motor. There were other types of insurance but they were a very small part of the business and any enquiries could be passed on to Dalby to be dealt with. Thankfully, as far as life policies were concerned, Dalby had trained up Judith, a worker in the other office, and any enquiries should be directed to her. That Thursday I spent the day under Dalby's tutelage. Helpfully there had been a broad range of enquiries that day so I was able to get a good feel for what I had to do to advise clients. Dalby paid frequent visits to the lavatory and I wondered if he shouldn't be at home but he insisted on staying and at the end of the day we travelled back to Saxmundham together. In the evening he seemed to have perked up considerably and was something like his usual self, mock boasting to Alice about his latest protégé. By the morning though he looked just as bad as ever and I tried to dissuade him from coming to the office. He insisted and I spent another day being schooled in the intricacies of insurance. In the Tacket Street office Judith dealt with life policy business while Ann was mainly concerned with the Dalby Apartment store. She was also responsible for the accounting side of things. Dalby had intended to base himself in the new office in Friars Street, where his new computer was and this is where I spent my two days a week. Each Thursday there was a backlog of queries to be dealt with. Most I could handle but there were also frequent calls to Dalby. In fact the women at Tacket Street and the new assistant in the Friars Street office, Siobhan, dealt with a great deal of stuff without ever having to consult me or Dalby. I had the feeling that Dalby was a bit old fashioned, seeing women more as auxiliaries to a business rather than principals. I felt that with more training and trust his female staff could probably manage the whole business.

In fact this new arrangement only lasted for a few weeks before Dalby became so ill that he couldn't get out of bed and was barely capable of using the phone such was his distress. He was in a complete panic about losing his business and becoming destitute. His fears were somewhat exaggerated but he was certainly a worried man. I felt I now had a good handle on the insurance business and decided to put a proposition to him. I went up to his bedroom. I thought I would come straight to the point.

'Adrian, are you able to pay me a salary?' Up to this point I had not been paid. Dalby had suggested an honorarium but I said it was unnecessary, not least because he was already providing me with board and lodging several days a week, and in London I was getting the same from Colette.

He looked puzzled: 'why do you ask?'

'I thought I might come and work for you full time, if that's what you wanted, but I would need my own place to live, hence the need for a salary. Once you get better you might like to keep me on and go into semi-retirement.'

I was being disingenuous. Dalby didn't look like a man who had much prospect of a recovery.

'Why couldn't you just stay here?'

'You haven't answered my question, though.'

'Well yes, I could certainly pay you. You really think you could manage?'

'I've picked up a lot these last couple of weeks. The girls are pretty knowledgeable and you're only at the end of the phone line. I reckon that between us we could do a good job.'

It was agreed, though Dalby still tried to persuade me to stay. I knew I couldn't. It was difficult enough staying three or four days. The sex with Alice had become perfunctory. It was my fault. Alice was as keen as ever but I felt increasingly guilty about cuckolding this sick man. When I told Alice what my plan was she seemed even more put out than Dalby. She was really quite insistent that I should stay living with them but I wouldn't be moved. I now had to find myself some accommodation. I didn't want and couldn't afford to rent a house or flat, even if any were available. A hotel would be hideously expensive. It seemed lodgings of some kind might be the answer. The one person I thought might be able to help was Angela at the church. Time for a chat.

'Still looking bright and cheerful, then,' was her slightly unexpected greeting.

'Mind reading again Angela?'

'No, but your appearance is now so different to when we first met. I take it things are going well, matters resolved. I'm a bit surprised that you're still in Saxmundham.'

'Not as surprised as me, though. Things have moved on. Bit of a long story but it looks like I'm going to be here for a while and I have a problem, something I hope you may be able to help me with. In fact if you can't, I have no idea where else to look.'

'I'm intrigued.'

'I need accommodation. I thought maybe you would know someone who would take in a lodger.'

'So are you working here now?'

'Yes, well, sort of. Bit difficult to explain. I'm helping someone out who's ill at the moment.'
'I think I might know someone. Give me a day or two.'
I called back in the evening of the next day. Angela explained that one of her congregation had been recently widowed. She knew that the woman would appreciate the extra income and had put to her the idea of taking in a lodger. She seemed keen and Angela had arranged for me to go round the following evening. Her name was Christine Davis. I needed to know more.
'What's she like this Christine? How old? Has she got children? What happened to her husband?'
'I would say she's in her early thirties. Two boys, primary school age. A quiet person, even quieter since her husband died. It was a car accident. It was his own fault, no-one else involved. Went round a bend too fast.'

20

Christine lived in a modern semi-detached house not far from the Dalbys. Nowhere in Saxmundham was very far from anywhere else. As I approached the front door it suddenly occurred to me that I hadn't asked Angela what she had told Christine about me. Did she I know I was an ex-con, for example? Too late to worry about that now, I rang the bell. The door opened almost instantly. I was slightly taken back by the appearance of the woman who answered it. Tall, with shoulder length blonde, wavy hair, dressed in a pale blue shirt and jeans. Stupid really. What did I expect – a woman in black, in floods of tears?

In my hesitancy she spoke first, 'Jim? Come in.'

She took me through to the living room. It was nicely set out with modern furniture, a TV in the corner, a large bookcase where a fireplace would have been. It was one of those through rooms which has windows at both front and back. At the far end at a table sat the two boys, involved in some kind of game. They gave me the briefest of glances before getting back to what they were doing.

I held out my hand which she took in a light grasp.

'Jim Mallinson. Angela says you might be able to take me as a lodger.'

'Yes, would you like to see the room?

We went upstairs and into the front bedroom. This had clearly been the matrimonial bedroom. Christine must have moved herself into one of the two smaller bedrooms. She stood there twisting her wedding ring on her finger and looking nervous, perhaps expecting me to say it wasn't what I was looking for.

'This is lovely, perfect.'

On the way downstairs we visited the bathroom and toilet. Back in the living room we stood facing each other. Neither of us seemed to know what to say next. We both started speaking at the same time, laughed, and the atmosphere relaxed a little. It was agreed that the rent would include breakfast and an evening meal, if I wanted it. Christine explained that she worked part-time in Saxmundham but was always back when the boys came out of school, so an evening meal would be no problem. She would get a key cut for me and I could move in the day after tomorrow. I took my leave and wandered back to Saxon Road in a bit of a daze. It all seemed so simple. She asked me nothing about myself, what I was doing in Saxmundham, how long I would be staying. Back at the Dalbys I broke the news. Alice looked piqued. I told her I would leave straightaway and get back down to London to see Colette and pick up my stuff. From there I would go straight to Christine's.

It being Friday I hoped Colette hadn't gone off to the country as she often did at weekends but she had. I spent a lonely Saturday, wandering round the West End. Somehow things looked different; pastel washed rather than the vivid colours that I remembered. Maybe it was the time of year or maybe it was just me. I hadn't really taken much time to think about what I was getting into. New job, living in a new place. In my haste I had forgotten that I would need to let the probation officer know and tell Simon. I hoped he wouldn't mind letting me go without notice. I had a very comfortable life in London. Did it make sense to give all this up to help out Dalby? After all what did he really mean to me? Had I got myself so wound up with Alice that I was no longer thinking straight? Impulsiveness had been my downfall. I didn't care to think that it might be so again. But what was there to fear? When I analysed it, there was nothing. Nevertheless, I seemed unable to get rid of a strange, murmuring dread at the back of my mind.

Sunday morning started with a bang. I came out of my bedroom to find Colette standing by the front door and her bag halfway down the hallway where she'd thrown it. She didn't look happy.
'Good weekend?'
'Those fucking morons. They are beyond stupid, beyond ignorant, beyond fucking-well being human!'
'Coffee?'
Colette came through to the kitchen where I made the coffee.
'Go on then. Seems like it was worse than normal.'
'It was. Geoffrey invited over a couple of his ex-soldier pals and their wives and one of their daughters. Inevitably the talk got round to politics. These people have no experience of the real world. They never meet people like the people I represent. People who've had no advantages in life, poorly educated, poorly parented; lost from birth, a lot of them. They think that because they've had it easy so has everyone else. They have no imagination.'
'Of course, in a way you're transcending the class gap.'
'What do you mean?'
'Well, you're from the same class as them but you gain insights through your work, by meeting people at the bottom of the pile. They don't have those opportunities.'
'But my grandfather wasn't like that. He was a lovely, caring, wise man. You know what the difference is? In those days he employed a lot of people. There were the servants in the house – that was really grandma's realm, but there were the estate workers, the tenant farmers and their families. Grandpa knew them all, the names of the children as well. He would often call by to see how they were getting on, and not beyond slipping them the odd pound or ten bob note. So he knew about people's lives, their problems and their little successes too. I know it was

paternalistic but it was better than some of the heartless attitudes we see today. Sorry I'm having a bit of a rant.'

'Not at all. It's interesting to hear what you have to say. What you describe is a world totally remote from mine. I think it's what they called the common touch, back then. Anyway, changing the subject I've got some news. I don't know if it's good or bad. I've got a job in Saxmundham, helping out a friend who's ill. I can't keep travelling back and forth so I've got myself some digs.'

'Is that what you want? Are you pleased?'

'I don't know. Everything happened in such a rush I didn't have time to think until yesterday. For some reason there's a little nagging doubt somewhere and I don't know why or what.'

'I'll miss you Jim. It's been nice to have someone in the flat.'

'Now you're making it worse. You've been so kind to me.'

'Not at all. It's cost me nothing and benefitted me plenty. But you'll come back for the odd weekend won't you? If you let me know when you're coming I'll make a point of not going down to the country. And keep the key. Come here anytime.'

So that was that. Now I just needed to tell Simon on Monday morning and pop in to the probation office. After that it was off to my new life.

It was on the Wednesday of the second week of my full-time job when Dalby appeared in the office. Siobhan had gone for lunch and I was entering records into the computer. I saw that someone had come in but I wanted to make the last few entries before getting up to deal whoever it was so I carried for a minute or so. When I looked up I barely recognised him. His appearance of health was almost as shocking as had been his death-mask the last time I saw him.

'Adrian, my God, you look wonderful. What happened?'

He laughed, 'I don't know. I seemed to start picking up as soon as you moved out.'

'That's it then. It must be like the curse of the mummy, only I'm the mummy. Don't come too close! Seriously have you seen the doctor? What does he say?'
'I did see the doctor but he was as clueless as me. He said it might have been an idiopathic disease.'
'What the hell is that?'
'Yes, he had to explain it to me too. It relates to a disease or condition that arises spontaneously with no known cause and it can also disappear spontaneously.'
'Well that's brilliant news. So I suppose you'll be coming back to work now and giving me the sack.'
'That's just what I won't be doing. These last few days as I've started to feel better I've had time to think. I don't know what caused this illness but maybe I was overdoing things; two offices and the Dalby Apartment Store side of things. So I've decided to try to have a more supervisory role. The business can easily accommodate your salary and I'm really pleased with the way you've cottoned on so quickly. You hardly ever need to consult me now. So your job is as safe as you want it to be.'
'Well, I hadn't imagined things turning out like this but I'm happy enough. I'm very comfortable with Christine and Saxmundham's a nice little place. Makes a pleasant change from London.'
I didn't see Dalby again until the following week when he came in several times. His health seemed to have sustained its improvement. He was putting on weight and the ruddiness was in his cheeks again. On the Thursday he invited me to come to dinner the following Saturday.

It's easy to tell when parents have done a good job raising their children. Christine's two boys, James who was eight and Harry who was six, were, it seemed to me, exceptionally well behaved for boys so young. They weren't repressed but went quietly about their business without any fuss. They helped out with household chores. Every morning James made sandwiches for his and his brother's lunch boxes. I got on OK with them but I wasn't about to take on the role of substitute father. Had I done so I know it would have been resented. I mentioned all this to Christine one time and she told me how much they had loved their father, who managed to combine being loving and caring with giving the boys a strong moral sense. As she told me all this she started to cry quietly and I felt awful for raising the subject. I apologised for upsetting her but she told me that I shouldn't. She was full of doubts about her capabilities a as a mother and it was good to hear what I had to say. I went to put an arm round her but at the same moment she started to move away and then as I withdraw my arm she realised what I was doing and apologised. It was an awkward moment, and not the last.

Christine and I got on very well. We chatted and occasionally laughed. In the evenings we were in the habit of watching television once the boys were in bed. We would sit on the sofa. She would turn on the television which I always prefaced with: 'what rubbish shall we watch tonight?' It was a friendly and comfortable routine. One evening after I had been staying for three weeks or so I felt a hand nestle into mine. It was not entirely a surprise but for me at that time it was unwelcome. I let her hand rest for a few moments before giving it a little squeeze and then moving my own hand away. Christine sat for a while longer before getting up and going out to the kitchen. I sat for ten minutes or so, looking at the television screen but with no idea what I was watching. What Christine might be experiencing as a rejection was in my mind something completely different. I could well imagine falling in love with this beautiful, kind and calm woman, and exactly because of that I could not enter into a physical relationship with her in such a light and casual way. I followed her into the kitchen. She was in a corner fiddling with some pots. Before I could say anything she started to apologise. I stopped her and apologised in my turn. I knew that long explanations would be neither wanted nor helpful at that moment. I simply said that my life was confusing and complicated at that moment and didn't want to make it more so, particularly at that risk of hurting somebody I was fond of. She nodded and busied herself with her pots and I took that as my signal to leave her alone. Things remained a little strained for a few days but we soon got back into our routine and nothing more was said.

The dinner party at the Dalbys was much like old times, though not entirely. Dalby looked almost back to normal he was a little thinner and his face hadn't quite returned to its rubicund norm. He was happy regaling us with his insurance stories. I particularly liked the story of the woman who put on her claim form that she ran a man down because he was taking too long on the crossing. Dalby trotted out these same old chestnuts at every dinner. I knew them by heart. Still, he was happy, dispensing his fine wines and generally acting the genial host. I liked Dalby. He was a simple man, who wanted to please people, particularly his wife. I was glad that he had recovered from his illness. Alice was quiet. She barely looked at me the whole evening. It seemed to me that the sexual side of our relationship might well be over. She had provided a splendid meal. There was smoked salmon to start, washed down with a nice Sancerre, followed by individual steak pies with all manner of vegetables. Dalby once more got out his expensive clarets for this part of the meal. Dessert was a strange concoction of meringue and fruit, and to have with this Dalby opened a bottle of champagne. When it came time to retreat to the living room I could barely move. I woke with a jump at the sound of a glass being broken. Dalby had got up and knocked his glass from the table. I looked at my watch. I must have been asleep for nearly an hour. I was glad that Christine's house was within easy staggering distance. Alice came to the door with me. She squeezed my arm and gave me a sly little smile. What did that mean?

<h1 style="text-align:center">21</h1>

It was Wednesday of the following week before I needed to consult Dalby. Alice answered and told me that Dalby had had a relapse and been taken to hospital. She told me that he had become ill on the Sunday but thought that the previous night's overindulgence might account for his malaise. By Monday the doctor had been called and he had been shipped off to hospital. It seems he was in Ipswich General, so I said I would call in after work. Dalby did not look at all good. He was wired up to various machines and drips and had an oxygen mask over his face. When he saw me he put out his hand to hold mine. He said nothing, merely squeezing my hand and shaking his head. There was nothing to be said. I told him I would call again tomorrow when I hoped he would be better. I caught hold of one of the doctors floating about. What did he think it was? He told me that they had no idea. They had run some tests but had not come up with anything conclusive.

By the time I called on Thursday evening Dalby was in a coma. The doctors didn't seem very hopeful that anything could be done. I rang Alice with the news but she had already spoken to the hospital.

'Don't you and the girls want to see him?' I asked.

'I don't think there's much point and it will be upsetting for the girls.'

'You could go by yourself and I would look after the girls.'
'Maybe I'll go down on Saturday.'
I thought to myself it will probably be too late by then, but said nothing. Alice didn't go on Saturday or any other day. Dalby hung on until Monday and died during that night. He had never regained consciousness. It was hard to concentrate on work, work that I had started doing to help Dalby. It all seemed pointless now. I told Alice that she would have to think about the future of Dalby's businesses and my role, if any. She was busy making funeral preparations. I carried on as normal, or as normal as it was possible to be with a great void looming ahead of me. I had no contact from Alice, although I had asked her to let me know the arrangements for the funeral. On the Tuesday of the week following Dalby's death two police officers came to the office. 'Mr Mallinson?'
'Yes.'
They showed me their warrant cards. One was tall and dark haired, smartly dressed with an extravagant moustache, about my age I guessed. He introduced himself as Sergeant Fellowes. The other was a rather short and dumpy female who he introduced as Detective Constable James.
'We would like to talk to you about the death of Mr Dalby.'
'What about it?'
'We'd prefer to talk to you at the station.'
'Well, I can't leave the office now. Is there some kind of problem?'
'As I say it would be better to talk at the station.'
'What about if I come along after work, about five? Where are you anyway?'
'In Museum Street'
They left, clearly unhappy at having to wait but there was nothing they could do. I phoned Alice. There was no reply. I spent all afternoon wondering what the problem might be. They would know of course that I had a record. A fact which gave me no comfort at all. The female officer was waiting for me in the foyer. She led me down a corridor to a small room where her

colleague was waiting. The room barely had space for its table and four chairs. On the wall next to the table was a tape recorder. There was no window. It felt oppressive.

Fellowes started the tape and spoke into it.

'What's with the tape recorder?'

'Standard procedure now when carrying out interviews, sir.'

We went through a few formalities establishing my name, address and so on.

'Can you tell me how you came to know Mr Dalby?'

'Whoa, hang on a minute. Before I answer any questions you better tell me what this is all about. You're making me feel like a criminal.'

'It would be better if you could just answer our questions.'

I got up. 'I'm going. You're not treating me like an idiot.'

'Please sit down Mr Mallinson.'

'No, not until you tell me why you are questioning me.' I remained standing. The two of them exchanged a glance and Fellowes nodded. Now the woman spoke.

'A post mortem was conducted last Friday and tests have shown that Mr Dalby was poisoned.'

'Poisoned how, by what?'

'Now can you see why we need to make enquiries?' This was Fellowes again.

'How was he poisoned?'

'We can't tell you that?'

They asked me how I had come to know the Dalby family, Alice in particular. I answered as honestly as I could. I didn't think it necessary to mention the recent sexual relationship with Alice. I left it that we were old friends from London days. Nothing more was said about the poisoning. It all seemed to be general background stuff. As I left they told me that they would probably want to speak to me again. The slight misgiving I had about Alice was growing into a menacing doubt. If Dalby really had been poisoned who else could have done it but she? But why? Certainly she would get hold of his businesses, what money he had. But what would that gain her? As it was Dalby would have given her anything she wanted. It didn't make any sense. Was she just mentally ill, a deranged psychopath? I had been a fool to ever go near her again.

For the next few days I tried to carry on as normal. Alice remained uncontactable. I speculated about calling round but then thought better of it. It came as no surprise when the police officers reappeared at the office about a week later. Would I come for another interview? Once more I refused to come until the office closed. This time I could see them hesitating, deciding whether to get heavy with me. In the end they accepted that I would see them after work. I was taken to the same interview room but there had been a change of personnel. The female officer remained but I was introduced to a new face, Inspector Lambert, a small thickset man with a pronounced belly which he struggled to contain in his trousers. His accent surprised me, quite upper class. It somehow didn't seem to fit his somewhat slovenly appearance. He gave me a broad smile and shook my hand. The female officer then cautioned me and asked me if I would like a solicitor.

'Why would I need a solicitor?' was my response.

The inspector spoke: 'Mr Mallinson, we believe that you have been involved in the poisoning of Adrian Dalby.'

'What! Absolute rubbish! Why would I do that? Dalby was very kind to me. I liked him.'

'Is it true that you have been having an affair with Mrs Dalby?'

'Yes, but Dalby knew about it, encouraged it.'

'Perhaps you thought that you could start a new life with Mrs Dalby, once her husband was out of the way.'

'I admit I had a sexual relationship with Alice but that's all it was. There was no romance there.'

'Didn't you tell Mrs Dalby that you longed to be with her permanently?'

'Absolutely not. Did she tell you that? If so, she's lying.'

'Didn't you say,' Here the inspector stopped to read from notes. '"Imagine if Adrian had an accident or fell ill, we could be together all the time"?'

'Complete rubbish.'

The inspector nodded to his colleague who produced a transparent evidence bag. It contained a bottle of weedkiller.

'Seen this before?'

'Yes Alice showed it to me. Asked me if it would be alright in the garden. That's the only time I've seen it.'

'You say Mrs Dalby showed it to you. That's interesting because her fingerprints are not on it but yours are.'

'When she showed it to me she was wearing her washing up gloves, her rubber gloves.'

'Really? It's true isn't it that Mr Dalby only started to become ill after you started the affair with Mrs Dalby.'

'Maybe, but a long time after.'

'And then after you stopped staying at the Dalbys, Mr Dalby recovered, almost completely in fact. Isn't that right?'

He continued: 'and then he became seriously ill, in fact terminally ill, after your most recent visit to the house.'

'This is Alice's doing, not mine. She's been very clever. Spun a web to trap me and a yarn to trap you. I had nothing to do with the poisoning of Dalby.'

'Strange then that it is your fingerprints that are on this bottle and not hers.'

'I've told you why.' But they were no longer listening. I was taken out and formally charged with Dalby's murder. Alice had been very clever and I had been exactly the opposite – a mug. How was this possible, that I was in the same position I had been in fifteen years ago? It was like a mad recurring nightmare. Last time I had put myself in the frame, with a little extra help from Alice. This time she had seen an opportunity. She had turned my reappearance to her advantage. There was I thinking that I was master when all the time she was in control – the puppet master. I asked to make a phone call. I knew I was entitled to this. I dialled Colette's number. I prayed that she would answer. Thank God, she did.

'Colette, please listen carefully. I've been charged with murder.'

'Jim that's not very funny.'

'Colette please, it's true. I'm at Ipswich police station now.'

'Whose murder?'

'The husband of the people I was staying with when I come up to Saxmundham. I'm supposed to have poisoned him. Can you help me?'

'I'm in the Bailey for the next two days. I can't get out of it but I'll come up after that. Where will you be?'

'They've just told me I'll be going to Chelmsford after my remand into custody tomorrow morning.'

'Right I'll make the necessary arrangements. Don't despair.'

But I was despairing. I could not face another term of imprisonment and I knew at that moment that I would certainly kill myself. The sounds and smells at the prison were all too familiar and I felt my morale sliding away as I went through processing. I was put in a cell with another remand prisoner. This was Julian. I would guess he was in his early sixties. He was a chatty type who despite my complete lack of response to his chatter continued relentlessly. He too was accused of murder, a murder which he freely admitted to. He had a tale to tell. During the war he had been in the merchant marine throughout. He spent his time on North Atlantic convoys and had been sunk three times. After the war he had had enough of the sea so settled down to become an insurance salesman. Things had gone well and he was able to afford a nice home and a good lifestyle for himself and his family. He had three children all born after the war although he had married in 1939 just before the war started. Two years ago he had taken retirement early and was looking forward to spending his time with his wife exploring Britain's countryside. They were both particularly interested in historic buildings. One day, in the pub Alan, one of his lifelong friends, had made a comment which seemed to indicate that he had known Julian's wife a lot better that he should have done. When challenged about this Alan pretended not to understand what he was getting at. Julian then challenged his wife who after a considerable brow beating finally agreed that she had had an affair with Alan while Julian was away at sea. For Julian this was the ultimate treachery. He felt that his whole life had been based on a lie. His wife tried to persuade him that it hadn't meant anything but he was not to be appeased and before he knew what he was doing he had strangled her. He said to me: "there she was, in my arms looking up at me, but dead." Julian was convinced that this was a crime of passion and that he would be let off. I didn't like to disillusion him. He said it over and over again. "It's a crime of passion. It's well known".

I had never seen Colette interact with anyone else before. She did so with charm and grace and the natural confidence of people of her class. It was fascinating to see the way that the prison officers deferred to her. It helped too that she was tall and beautiful. I had the feeling that the warders would do anything she asked. She had come on the Thursday as she had promised. I was waiting for her in a little grey-painted room, bare of furniture except for a much scrawled on wooden table and two metal chairs. A window high up above the table gave the only natural light.

'How are you Jim?'

'Glad to see you, that's for sure.'

'You're going to have to tell me the whole story, right from the beginning. No need to tell me about your trial. I read the transcript while I was hanging about at the Bailey.'

'Yes but there's something the transcript won't tell you. Alice came to see me when I was in Pentonville. She confessed that she had killed Laura. It seems they were lovers. They were both bisexual and there was some sort of jealous argument when they were both drunk and Alice had hit her with the decanter. She hadn't meant to kill her. The rest you know. So you see she's now killed twice.'

'Yes but you're getting ahead of yourself. I want to know everything that's happened since you left prison.'

So I set it all out. The whole story of tracking Alice down; the thoughts of revenge which had strangely evaporated; the strange sexual affair and then Dalby's illness and death.

'My God Jim, why did you ever go near her again?'
I didn't answer. I didn't need to. Colette went on: 'So their case amounts to a fingerprint and some shaky circumstantial evidence. I don't think the CPS will be happy with that.'
'Well I guess since it's so clear he was murdered they've got to be seen to be prosecuting someone.'
'I wonder if they even looked at Alice as the perpetrator.'
'She's very clever. She's probably told them a whole pack of lies about my involvement, my wish to see Dalby dead, all that kind of stuff.'
'OK. Now listen. I will take your case but you can't instruct me. You will have to get your solicitor to do that. I'm assuming you don't have anybody so I will get someone I know to come and see you. The contact will be through him or her. Once we've got a trial date and we've seen the prosecution case we'll know how to go on. And like I say, don't despair. We'll get this sorted out.' She stood up to go. I did likewise and we embraced. I felt my eyes misting up and found it difficult to speak. I started to say something but she put her finger over my lips and then kissed me and then she was gone.

The next few months were miserable in the extreme. The only relief was brought by visits from Christine. Although she hardly knew me she believed completely in my innocence and displayed a loyalty to this foolish man that was quite undeserved. With the two boys to look after, her visits were rare. I didn't contact anyone else, by which I meant Steve, who was the only person likely to visit me. I felt ashamed. Ashamed to have got myself in this ridiculous position once again. After about two months I had a surprise visit from Angela. Christine had told her what had happened. She was very positive.
'I won't tell you that I've been praying for you Jim as I know that means nothing to you.'
'Don't be so sure about that Angela. It's nice to know somebody cares.'

'Of course I care and Christine does too, very much. She's very fond of you, you know.'
She let the implied continuation hang.
'Then she's mad. A bloody fool twice over, that's me. She deserves something better.'
Angela ignored that and we went on to chat about prison life and about anything and nothing; about her work and her congregation and her dream to become ordained. She was easy to be with and lifted my spirits. When it was time for her to go she told me she wanted to say a little prayer with me. When she had finished I thanked her and asked her if she thought I was getting religion. She laughed and tweaked my nose. There goes a woman entirely good. How odd that the world can contain people such as her and others entirely bad.

Julian's case came to trial during my stay at Chelmsford. He was to be disappointed in his expectation of having been found to have committed a crime of passion, as he so often averred, but he got second best when the jury rejected the charge of murder and found him guilty of manslaughter. There was clearly some sympathy for the situation he had found himself in. He got five years, and with the time he had already served and full remission, he would be out in two.
I was hoping my new cell mate would be as easy to be with as had been Julian. I was not to be disappointed, although initially I was extremely apprehensive when I saw the new arrival. Two days after Julian had left to go to his new prison another remand prisoner moved in. This was Boris, short, thickset and tattooed; in his late twenties I thought. Boris liked to take his shirt off whenever possible to give me the benefit of admiring his collection of tattoos. I asked him one day, why the tattoos. He looked at me for a long time but didn't answer. The following day he asked me why I had asked him the question. I told him I was just curious and then he finally admitted that he didn't know why he had got them. He went on:

'I'm like that. I don't know why I do things. Sometimes I do things because other people do them. I got married when I was eighteen. I didn't even like her but she kept on at me. She told me I had to marry her because I'd fucked her. We had no money so we had to live with her mum and dad. They chucked me out after six months. Then my mate Faz joined the army so I did. Did three years. Hated it. I got out but Faz stayed in. Now I'm in this shithole.'

Boris had been charged with GBH. He'd had a drunken row with someone in a pub and ended up glassing the other man. At first I was scared of him but as the weeks went by I became quite fond of him. I was so different to him that I was no threat, and he seemed to enjoy talking to me about himself. Like a thousand others in every prison he had had a terrible childhood. No love and little attention had taught him that the only way he could get anywhere was by shouting or being violent, often both. I guessed he was not unintelligent but had been such a nuisance at school that the teachers were happy when he played truant, which was most of the time. Inevitably he teamed up with other youngsters of the type and spent his time shoplifting, breaking into cars and generally vandalising anything he came across. There was a deep seated anger in him that would need years of therapy to control; therapy that he was never likely to receive. Instead he would spend his life being a nuisance to society just as he had been a nuisance to his school. He was one of four. His brother had ended his career as a drug dealer with a bullet in the head, and one of his sisters was following their mother, having drunken sex with any number of different men. The eldest of the children, his sister Amy, was the sensible one, he told me. It was she that he went to when things started to get on top of him, which was often. I felt sorry for this man, someone, who outside of prison, I would probably be scared of but with him in the cell I only felt pity for. He was like a small angry child in an adult's body. His trial came up quite quickly. He pleaded guilty and got two and a half years. And then it was my turn.

22

I had had several meetings with Colette and my solicitor before the trial date. Once she had seen the prosecution's case she was confirmed in her opinion that the case against me was weak. The principal witness, in fact the only witness apart from the police and the technical experts was Alice.

Christine remained ever faithful. She wrote to me often and shortly before the trail managed a visit and brought me a suit. It was one of her husband's and fitted me very well. I was touched.

I hardly slept at all before the first day of the trail. I was up and ready hours before being collected and taken to Ipswich Crown Court. The case had attracted a fair bit of attention and the public gallery was full. The first day of the trial was taken up with the swearing in of the jury and the opening speeches of the prosecution and defence. It seemed to me a lot of time was taking up with procedural matters and unnecessary adjournments. It didn't surprise me that modern trials take so long. There seemed to be a conspiracy between all the professionals to make things proceed in the most dilatory manner possible. I had read about murder trials back in Victorian times being completed in a day.

As I came into court on the second day I caught sight of Christine in the public gallery and next to her Angela. I was deeply touched that these two women, who I hardly knew, had come to support me. I smiled up at them and got a little wave back. That morning the consultant from Ipswich General gave his evidence. He described the course of Dalby's illness through the period when he was being regularly ill and then his final illness on the Sunday after I had visited. Next was the pathologist who described the finding of the weedkiller in Dalby's organs. He confirmed that he had been poisoned over a long period. Next came an expert on poisons who described the appearance and chemical composition of the weedkiller. In her cross examination Colette asked about the taste of the weedkiller. She first wanted to know if it would be noticeable in a drink. He confirmed that it definitely would. Next she asked how noticeable it would be in a highly flavoured food. He thought that it might not be noticeable, depending on the quantity used. She finally asked if it might be noticeable in a steak pie. The expert was unable to say. There was some muttering in the public gallery. No doubt there was some discussion as to the relevance of a steak pie.

On the third day it was Alice's turn. She was dressed in a black suit and was wearing a small pill box hat with a tiny veil, clearly the grieving widow still. Nevertheless, I had to admit she looked very nice. Counsel first asked her about the period when she had lived in London and how she had come to know me. He asked her how long the relationship had lasted and then asked her how the relationship had ended. Colette shot out of her seat and called out: 'objection'.

'What is your objection Miss Montague-Brown?'

'If Mr Bass continues with this line of questioning he will undoubtedly cause a mistrial. May I speak to your honour in chambers.'

The judge adjourned the case and ordered both the lead counsels to his chambers. I realised what the point was. If Alice had answered the question, as she would have done, by saying that the relationship had ended when I was sent to prison for murder it would inevitably prejudice the outcome of the present case and cause a mistrial.

When they returned Mr. Bass was looking very red in the face and Colette bore a wry smile. She whispered to me: 'the judge has given old Bass a right bollocking.' Colette's use of such a word made me smile. It was so totally out of character.

'Before you continue Mr Bass I must warn you that any repetition of this kind of prejudicial questioning will result in your dismissal from the court.'

So, a small victory for the defence. Bass then took Alice through our renewed acquaintance. There was no mention of the confrontation when I had asked her to strip. She just told the court that I had turned up one day out of the blue. She went on to say that I had befriended Dalby and thereby insinuated myself into their life. I had then pressurised her into restarting a sexual relationship. In a moment of weakness she had given in and thereafter had had to submit, feeling that I had always the threat of telling Dalby hanging over her, if she did not. She went on to say that I had often remarked what a good time we might have if Dalby suddenly died, telling her that she would be a rich woman, that we could start a new life together. She of course had been horrified at the idea.

Bass then led her on to the period of Dalby's illness, emphasising the point that it had started during my frequent visits to the house. He got her to describe in detail the course of the illness and how awful it had been for Dalby, how much he had suffered, and the failure of the medical services to find out what was wrong with him. None of this description was in any way germane to the matter of proof. It was simply the prosecution building up a picture of the horror of the crime that had been committed. Colette, I noticed, listened carefully, while making notes, occasionally nodding to herself and on one occasion whispering, 'got you'.

Alice then recounted, at Bass's prompting, how during the period when I was no longer staying at the house, Dalby had made an almost miraculous recovery. This period of recovery suddenly being ended after my last visit to the house on the occasion of the Saturday evening meal. I thought it interesting that Bass didn't ask Alice to go into the details of the meal. It could only be because he felt that there was a weakness there.

Colette stood up to cross examine. She was holding a pair of glasses. The last time I had seen her wear them was on the train from Aylsham I suspected the glasses were a prop as much as anything else. Once she had stood up she took her time looking at her notes, the glasses perched on the end of her nose. She then took them off and smiled at Alice. I sensed that this was all part of an act to discomfit the witness.

'Mrs Dalby, when was the last time you had sex with your husband?'

Bass immediately objected. The judge asked the reason for this line of questioning.

'I wish to establish the nature of the sexual relationship between my client and this witness, which I believe is not as the witness has stated.'

The judge gave her leave to continue.

'Very well, Mrs Dalby, what is your answer?'

'I can't remember.'

'Was it not in fact more than five years ago, when you became depressed following the birth of your second child?'

'It might have been. I can't remember.'

'Didn't you tell my client…' She paused, put on her glasses and read from her notes.

'Didn't you tell my client that you had ceased having sexual relations with your husband at that time, and you said, and I quote, "he wasn't very good anyway. I usually had to finish myself off", didn't you say that?'

There was a stirring in the court.

'No of course not.'

'On the 11 June 1990, the first occasion when you had sex with my client didn't you initiate intercourse by saying..'

Again the dramatic pause and the consulting of notes, glasses perched precariously.

'…"I want you to fuck me. Please fuck me".'

'No he's lying.'

What instinct of self-preservation caused me to keep the note that Alice had written on that day I cannot say. It was never a conscious thought, more an inadvertent act of tidiness, when I had put it away in a drawer in Colette's flat. Possibly there always remained a tiny node somewhere in my brain sparking away and saying 'don't trust this woman'.

Colette had the note in an evidence bag. She read it out.

'Did you write that?'

There was no answer and Colette gave the note to an usher to show to Alice.

'Is that not your writing and your signature?'

Alice's calm demeanour had disappeared completely by now. Her face was an ugly mask of red and white blotches.

'Why are you asking me all these questions? There's the murderer.'

'Would you answer the question? Is that your handwriting and signature? I should advise you that these things can be checked by a handwriting expert and you are still under oath. Well?'

Alice looked towards the judge, perhaps hoping to be saved from what was becoming a nightmare. He provided no consolation but told her she had to answer the question.

'Yes', she whispered.

'Can you repeat your answer so the court can hear?'

'Yes', she almost shouted.

'So when you told counsel for the prosecution that it was my client who had pressurised you into a relationship and then held it over you, it was a lie, wasn't it. It was in fact you who had started the relationship. It was you who had pressurised my client into starting an affair.'

'If you like.'

'Not if I like Mrs Dalby. This is nothing to do with what I or anybody else likes. This is about the truth.'

Colette had done a good job in damaging, if not destroying Alice's credibility. She wasn't finished.

'I want to move on now to May 17 1991, the occasion on which it is alleged that weedkiller was given to Mr Dalby by my client.

The prosecution alleged in their opening remarks that the weedkiller was in some way administered to Mr Dalby's food during that evening meal to which my client was invited. Can you describe the meal Mrs Dalby?'

'It was smoked salmon, followed by steak pie with various vegetables and then a pudding called Eton Mess.'

'How was the smoked salmon served? Was it on a shared dish from which those present helped themselves or was it served on individual plates.'

'On a dish.'

'And what about the vegetables and the dessert, served individually or from a common dish?'

'From dishes.'

'Now tell us about the steak pie.'

'It was just a steak pie.'

'Were there not individual steak pies?'

'I can't remember, maybe.'

'Really? Perhaps I can jog your memory. Did you not bring in from the kitchen three individual steak pies, one of which you served to my client, one to your husband, and one to yourself?'

Alice didn't want to answer this, sensing the trap. She again looked towards the judge but received no help there.

'Mrs Dalby, the court is waiting for your answer.'

'Well yes, I think it was like that.'

'That being the case, it is clear, is it not, that if the poison had been administered in the food, it could not have been administered in the food which was shared communally, otherwise everybody would have been poisoned. Therefore the weedkiller could only have been in the steak pie that your husband ate, the steak pie that you prepared?'

'Are you implying that I killed my husband?'

'I'm implying nothing. Merely coming to the logical conclusion that whoever poisoned your husband almost certainly did so by he or she putting the poison in your husband's steak pie.'

'It might have been done another way.'

'Thank you. I was coming to that. The weedkiller is sold in a bright red plastic bottle, is it not? Did you see my client with such a bottle during the meal?'

'No.'

'Did you see my client put anything into your husband's food or in his drink?'

'No, but I wasn't there all the time.'

'Indeed, you were in the kitchen preparing the meal no doubt, but one would imagine that Mr Dalby might have noticed if my client had produced a bright red bottle and poured some of it into his drink or onto his food.'

This final little speech caused a ripple of restrained laughter from the public gallery.

When it had subsided Colette merely said, 'no further questions.'

I was surprised that Bass didn't re-examine Alice. Maybe he thought it might make matters worse.

Alice's evidence and cross-examination had taken up most of the day and the judge didn't want the prosecution to call another witness late in the afternoon, so the trial was once more adjourned.

On the Friday morning Inspector Lambert described the police investigation. Alerted by the post mortem report, he and a colleague had interviewed Mrs Dalby. Her report of statements made by the defendant then led them to interview him. A search of the Dalby home had led to the discovery of the bottle of weedkiller, a subsequent examination of which revealed the accused's fingerprints. This was in essence the prosecution case; the fingerprints together with Dalby's illness coinciding with my visits to the house.

Colette took her time in standing, up riffling through her notes, and removing and putting on her glasses several times. She gave the inspector her most charming smile before beginning: 'not very much is it inspector?'

There was no answer he could or was expected to give to what was a rhetorical question but I could see that the message had got through to him; that he was going to have an uncomfortable time in the next few minutes.

'You say that searched the Dalby home, inspector. How many rooms did you search?'

'We searched the spare bedroom.'

'No other rooms then.'

'No.'

'Why was that?'

'We understood that that is where the defendant used to sleep.'

'So you had already formed the conclusion that it was my client who had carried out the poisoning, despite the fact that at that time you had no concrete evidence. Is that correct?'

'We had spoken to Mrs Dalby about the conversation that she had had with the defendant.'

'Did you think at any time that Mrs Dalby herself might be the perpetrator of this crime?

'Yes.'

'And what did you do about it?'

'We interviewed her.'

'How many times did you interview her?'

'Once.'

'And after that one interview you were quite happy that she was innocent and that you should turn your attention to my client?'

'It seemed very probable to us that it was the accused who had been involved in the poisoning.'

'And now you needed evidence and Mrs Dalby was about to provide you with that evidence. Is that not so?'

'We found the evidence when we searched the spare bedroom.'

'Yes, the spare bedroom to which Mrs Dalby directed you. When you say you searched the bedroom do you actually mean that Mrs Dalby showed you where the bottle of weedkiller was?'

'It was in a wardrobe.'

'How well hidden was it?'

'It was on a shelf.'

'In plain view?'

'Yes.'

'So not hidden at all, in fact. So what do we have so far? Mrs Dalby tells you about comments that my client said to her, and we only have her word for that, and then she leads you to the bottle of weedkiller. Did it occur to you inspector that in fact you were being manipulated by Mrs Dalby, who was busy covering her own tracks by implicating someone else? Now this bottle of weedkiller. What was found when it was examined?'

'The defendant fingerprints were found.'

'And what other fingerprints?'

'None.'

'None? Rather unusual wouldn't you say, inspector? What about the people who would have handled the bottle in the factory or in the shop, or potential customers looking at the bottle. Where were their fingerprints?'

'There weren't any.'

'Is that usual? Is it usual that a bottle that has been certainly handled by a number of people has only one set of fingerprints? How do you explain that inspector?'

'I can only tell you what was found when the bottle was examined.'

'So you have no explanation. Now you tell us that my client's fingerprints were found on the bottle. How many sets of his fingerprints were there?'

'Just the one set.'

'Isn't that also rather odd? It is alleged that my client poisoned Mr Dalby over a period of time, which would mean he must have handled the bottle on a number of occasions. Surely his fingerprints would have been all over the bottle but you say there is only one set. How can that be?'

'I can only repeat what I said before and tell you what was found.'

'So once again you have no explanation for this what one might say is an impossible situation. No further questions.'

By the time he came off the stand the inspector was looking very uncomfortable. He was red in the face and sweating. As he stepped down he blew hard and loosened his collar. Colette was also a little flushed but I think well satisfied with her work. There being no more prosecution witnesses the judge decided that the presentation of the defence case would wait until the following Monday, this being Friday.

Back in my cell I asked Colette how she thought it was going. She felt that she had made a very severe dent in the prosecution case, which as she reiterated was weak to start with. We went through my testimony for the Monday. All you need to do is tell the truth and not embellish, not extemporise, she told me. She also said that she was going to call two other witnesses but wouldn't tell me who they were.

Called to the witness box on Monday morning I was happy and reassured to see Christine and Angela once more. Colette took me through my story from my re-acquaintance with Alice right through to the moment of my arrest. She particularly focused on my relationship with Dalby.

'What was your opinion of Mr Dalby?'

'I thought he was a kind-hearted, fairly simple kind of man.'

'Can you explain what you mean?'

'It seemed to me that he wanted little from life apart from the ability to provide for his family and earn their love and respect. The fact he encouraged me to have a sexual relationship with his wife demonstrated what an extraordinary love he must have felt for her.'

'Now, that relationship came to an end, did it not, while you were still visiting and staying at the Dalby home. Why was that?'

'It somehow didn't seem right to be having sex with the wife of a man who was so ill, who was suffering so much under the same roof. I couldn't do it.'

'And what was the attitude of Mrs Dalby?'

'She wanted to continue.'

This brought another round of muttering in the public gallery.

'Now during this period of Mr Dalby's illness I believe you started working for him in his insurance business. Is that correct?'

'Yes for two days a week.'
'And why was that?'
'I wanted to help out in some way. Mr Dalby had been so kind to me and I liked him. I thought it was the least I could do.'
'How much were you paid?'
'I didn't want any payment. The Dalbys were providing me with accommodation and food while I was working so it wasn't necessary and when I was in London I was also provided for.'
Colette raised an eyebrow.
'Later you started working full-time. Why was that?'
'Mr Dalby became very seriously ill and was capable of doing very little. He was very worried about losing his business. By that time I had got a good idea of the business and felt I could get by with only the minimum of help from him.'
'But you moved out of the Dalby home into lodgings. Why was that?'
'I felt it would be an imposition to be staying there full-time. Until that point I had been coming up from London and staying two or three nights. I didn't think staying all the time was practicable or fair on the Dalbys.'
'What was their attitude?'
'They wanted me to stay.'
'Both Mr and Mrs Dalby?'
'Particularly Mrs Dalby.'
'Now I want to come to Exhibit 4, the bottle of weedkiller. Have you seen that bottle before?'
'Yes.'
'When was that?'
'It would be about the middle of December. I was at the Dalby's house and Mrs Dalby gave me the bottle to look at.'
'Why did she do that?'
'She asked me if I thought it would be suitable for her garden.'
'And what was your reaction?'
'I was slightly amused as I know nothing about gardening.'
'So what did you do?'

'I read the label and told Mrs Dalby that as far as I could tell it would be OK.'

'What did you do then?'

'I gave the bottle back to her.'

'Now, evidence has shown that your fingerprints are on the bottle. Can you explain why those of Mrs Dalby are not?'

'Well at that time she gave the bottle to me she was wearing rubber gloves, her washing up gloves.'

Colette always finished her examinations with an unanswered question hanging in the air. She was artful and I could see why she enjoyed her work and was reluctant to give it up, despite not needing the money.

Bass made a long theatrical pause, shuffling his notes, before looking up at me.

'Pretty story isn't it, Mr. Mallinson. Or should I say an unbelievable story.'

Colette had warned me that Bass would try and rile me, get me flustered and look a less than reliable witness. I felt that his question needed no answer from me so said nothing.

'What do you say?'

'I'm not sure what your question is.'

'I suggest to you that what you have told this court is a fiction, is that not so?'

'No, I've told the truth.'

'You are asking this court, this jury…' he pointed to them, 'to believe that the late Mr Dalby encouraged you to have sex with his wife.'

'Well, that's the truth.'

'Come now, Mr Mallinson, is it not the case that you pressured Mrs Dalby to have sex with you and then threatened her with exposure if she didn't continue to give into your demands.'

'It's as I said.'

Colette had warned me not to bring up the note. She would cover this fully in her summing up. If I mentioned it to Bass it would give him the chance to say that it had been written under duress.

'You say that you became involved in Mr Dalby's insurance business to help him out when he became ill. Was it not the case that what you were actually doing was inveigling yourself into his affairs so that you would be in a better position to take over the business after you had killed him?'

'No, what happened was just as I have said.'

I was realising by now that this cross-examination was not a series of questions that needed answers but rather a series of statements for the jury's benefit. A reminder of the prosecution's case. I just needed to be patient.

'Mr Mallinson how did it feel to be watching a man slowly die, a man you had poisoned.'

'I didn't poison him. I think you need to look elsewhere.'

As soon as I said it, I realised it was a mistake. Bass realised too.

'Oh so you're accusing someone else are you. Trying to shift the blame. Perhaps you're accusing Mrs Dalby; this poor lady whom now has to bring up her children without the love and support of her husband. Is that what you're saying?'

'It's not for me to say. I'm only saying it was not me.'

'Indeed, it is not for you to say. It is for those who uphold the law in this country to say, and they have decided, without any doubt, that the perpetrator of this evil crime is you. No further questions.'

Colette didn't re-examine, nor did she look at me as I went back to the dock. I felt that I had made a blunder in giving Bass an entrée.

I wondered who these two witnesses were that Colette had decided to call. I couldn't think who else might have anything to say or information to impart, so it was a surprise when I saw Siobhan from the office called. Colette first established that she worked for Dalby in one of the Ipswich offices and that in the recent past she had worked alongside me.

'Mrs Kelly I want to ask you about a conversation that you had with Mr Mallinson when you were working together. I believe you began by asking how he knew Mr Dalby. Is that correct.'

'Yes I asked him that and he told me that he had met him through his wife, who was an old friend.'
'And I believe you asked my client his opinion of Mr Dalby.'
'Yes I did.'
'And what did he say?'
'That he had been impressed by his warmth and kindness, and when he became ill he felt he wanted to do something to help out.'
'Did he say anything else?'
'He said that it was unusual these days to meet someone who seemed to have no negative side. He thought Mr Dalby was a simple man who loved his wife and adored his children. He said he was very fond of him but he wasn't sure that his wife was equally so.'
'So let me be quite clear. My client expressed his affection for Mr Dalby but he had doubts about his wife's feeling for him; that is Mr Dalby?'
'That's right.'
'And I also want to be clear that it was you who initiated this conversation. These were not unsolicited remarks by my client. Is that correct.'
'Yes.'
Bass didn't cross-examine, unsurprisingly. Colette then called the next witness. It turned out that this was a fingerprint expert form a private forensic science laboratory. Once she had established her credentials she took her through her evidence.
'Miss Gardner you undertook some research on behalf of the defence. Can you describe that research?'
'I purchased six bottles of Weed-All weedkiller from three different shops. Using gloves I placed them in evidence bags and returned to the laboratory where they were tested for fingerprints.'
'Let me be clear, you didn't handle these bottles yourself other than with gloves.'
'Correct.'
'And what were your findings?'

'All the bottles had multiple fingerprints on them. Many were smudged but it was clear that in every case at least two people had handled the bottles and in three cases at least three.'

'So in your opinion, any bottle of this weedkiller purchased in the normal way would have a similar pattern of fingerprints, even before those of the purchaser were added?'

'Yes'

Bass got up to cross-examine. I suddenly had an ominous feeling.

Miss Gardner, thinking here about Exhibit 4, the bottle of weedkiller, which we have already heard has just the defendant's fingerprints on it, would such a pattern be found if the person using that weedkiller had wiped it clean and then inadvertently touched it again?'

'Yes, I suppose it would.'

'Thank you. No further questions.'

There being no further defence witnesses the judge adjourned the trial for the day.

Colette did not look up from her notes. Junior counsel tried whispering something to her but she pushed him away. She was not happy and neither was I. We had shot ourselves in the foot, or possibly somewhere higher. She had been too clever. She came down to the cell. She was flushed.

'I'm sorry Jim. I never thought of that.'

I couldn't be angry with her. She had done so much for me.

'Well, all isn't lost, is it?'

'No, no. My point about the fingerprints is still valid. It carries less weight now though after Bass's cross-examination. It's still altogether a weak case.'

Not so weak now, I thought, but didn't say.

'What happens next?'

'Tomorrow we will make our closing speeches and the judge will sum up. Then it's up to the jury.'

'Will there be a verdict tomorrow?'

'There should be, if the jury have got any sense.'

A recurring nightmare tortured me throughout the night. In it, the jury returns. None of them look at me. They give their verdict – guilty. Before sentencing the judge asks –'anything known?' The clerk stands up, 'found guilty of murder 1975, life imprisonment, fourteen years served.' There is a collective gasp from the public gallery. A voice louder than the others says, 'he's done it before.' I shout at him, 'no it wasn't me', and I wake up still shouting. I must have had the dream a dozen times and in the morning I'm exhausted. I feel resigned. At the court Colette notices my state.

'Jim you've got to perk yourself up. The jury mustn't see you like that. You're like a man who's already been condemned.'

'I feel like it.' The well of my confidence was never filled very high and now the last drops had been drained away.

Bass's closing speech contained no surprises. He reiterated again the two hooks from which the Crown's case was suspended. He made little mention of Alice's evidence. Colette on the other hand took her testimony apart. She pointed out emphatically how she had been caught lying and suggested that this should cast doubt on the rest of her evidence. She described the prosecution case as being so weak that a prosecution should never have been brought, and she said with emphasis, at least against this person. I thought it was a telling point. I only hoped the jury shared my view.

The judge's summing up seemed to me to state the case exactly. If the jury felt that the fingerprints and the coincidence of the timing of Dalby's illness convinced them then the verdict was guilty. I noticed that he was rather dismissive of Alice's evidence, undoubtedly because she had been caught in a lie – the crucial piece of paper.

By now it was lunchtime. The judge told the jury that they should have their lunch and then stay out until, they had reached a verdict. By four o'clock there was no news. Colette was down with me. I asked her was it good or bad that they were taking so long. She couldn't say. It seems that the length of time the jury was out was not a determiner of the nature of the verdict. She told me that it was often the case that one or two jurors took a contrary view to the others and couldn't be persuaded to alter their views. This was why majority verdicts had been brought in.

At five o'clock the message came. The jury were returning. They came back in. Several of them looked at me. One woman smiled. Surely that was a good sign. The judge asked me to stand. I could barely do so. My legs were shaking, my mouth was dry, I felt light-headed. I had to grip the rail in front of me. One of the prison officers took my elbow. 'Steady mate.' I muttered a thank you. I didn't hear what the jury foreman said. I thought I heard 'not guilty'. I turned to the prison officer, 'did they say not guilty?' He smiled, 'yes mate'. And then my knees went and I found myself falling on to the chair behind me, and then sliding off on to the floor. I was hoisted back up on to the chair, shaking like a leaf. The judge was saying that he agreed with the jury's verdict; that he recommended that the police look at the whole case once again. The court started to empty. It took me a few minutes to recover myself. I was helped down from the dock. There was Colette. We embraced. I said nothing. She knew. Christine and Angela came into the court. I embraced them both and then I had to sit again and I then I started to cry, great howling sobs. In between, I incoherently thanked them over and over, told them I loved them, that I didn't deserve them, I didn't deserve their love. They started to laugh, the three of them, calling me a soft sausage, a silly boy who didn't know what he was talking about. In the end I had to join in their laughter. It was after all an expression of the relief they felt after being under so much pressure. Concentrating on myself I had forgotten what they too had been through. We walked out into the rain, rain I had never been so glad to feel on my face. Christine and Angela were going to take me home, home to Saxmundham. I started to say something to Colette.

'It's alright Jim. Get yourself together. Take a rest. Give me a ring when you feel like it.'

I muttered my thanks once again and then we got into Angela's car. We drove. It was like the day I first went for that walk with Julia. The green of leaves, never so green; the little flowers like bright points of light through the sward; the great white clouds towering up one upon the other. I wondered if I was suffering from a visual disturbance; everything was so vivid as to seem almost artificial. I remembered as a child seeing The Wizard of Oz and being shocked at the intense luminosity of the colours, such a contrast to the greys and browns of 1950s Britain. And here it was happening again, but without a cinema screen. We drove on through the chaotic prettiness of the English countryside, each new panorama a treat for my prison eyes. Back in Saxmundham Christine had prepared a meal in anticipation of the right verdict. She collected her boys from a neighbour and we sat down to eat. Angela had brought some wine. The first glass loosened my tongue and I started telling them again how little I deserved their kindness, and so on. Once again they told me to shut up and we all laughed.

23

Christine was calling my name. I woke with a start. For a moment I had no idea where I was but then her face came into focus and I realised that I had fallen asleep on the sofa. She took my arm and led me up the stairs. I started to thank her all over again until she put her fingers over my lips.

'Get some sleep Jim. Tomorrow is another day.'

It may have been another day but it was half gone by the time I woke up. The house was empty. Of course it would be. Christine had to work. She had taken part of her holiday entitlement in order to attend the trial, I later found out. She had left the breakfast things out and a note telling me when she would be back. She reminded me that I still had my own front door key should I need to go out. Typically, of course, I had continued my lifelong habit of never thinking more than five minutes ahead. In this case no further than the end of the trial. Although that was not entirely true. I had determined that if the verdict was guilty I would end it all but I had never dared think about the alternative. Now I had to. I had no job, no income. I had two places to live. With Colette where I could live for free and with Christine where I couldn't. Much as I loved Colette, and I use that word correctly, it was not romantic love, despite our occasional sexual encounters, but love nevertheless. I loved her for the person she was, so kind and generous. But I didn't want

186

to stay in London. I had grown fond of Saxmundham. I liked its smallness, its intimacy, its lack of rush and bustle. I wanted to explore the countryside hereabouts, that English countryside with which I was so little familiar. I supposed Christine might encourage me to stay but to do so long term without being able to make a contribution would be morally wrong. As a lodger I was meant to be there to supplement her income, not subtract from it.

I thought a walk might clear my head, give me a chance to think. I found myself on the road where Bert lived. I'd enjoyed my chat with him, so perhaps time to call again. The front garden wasn't quite as neat as it had been and I noticed his rose bush needed deadheading. I hoped these weren't ominous signs. I rapped the door several times. I knew it would be unlocked so eventually I pushed it open. I called out. Nothing. A peek into the living room showed everything in order. I walked through to the kitchen and then out into the garden. Bert was sitting on a chair by his vegetable patch.

'Bert?'

'Christ, you made me jump.'

'Sorry Bert. I knocked on the door.'

'Yes, I'm getting a bit deaf, and a bit old, alright, very old. Struggling now with these veg. Thinking of grassing it over and finishing with the veg for good.'

'That would be a pity.'

'Yes, but what can you do? Got to face facts.'

'I'd help you but I know nothing about gardening. I know quite a lot about weedkiller.'

'It's mainly common sense and…' He stopped mid-sentence and turned towards me, turned back to look at the ground, thought for a moment and then turned back to me again.

'So it was you. I thought I recognised your picture in the paper. Well, well. I'm glad you got off. What I want to know is what the police are doing about that woman.'

'Mrs Dalby. Yes, I'd like to know too. Nothing, probably.'

Bert couldn't quite get over linking me and the man on trial. He kept repeating 'well, well', almost as though it was helping him digest the fact. Eventually he seemed able to move on.

'So you staying on in Saxmundham then?'

'I'd like to but I have no job and no money.'

'The council's looking for someone. You could go after that. They've been looking for ages. Can't get anybody. Money's rubbish of course.'

'I'm afraid they wouldn't employ me with my history.'

'But you've been cleared.'

'I'm not talking about that. There's something else in my murky past.'

'Go on then.'

'It's a long story.'

'Alright, tell you what. Let's have a cup of tea. You can tell me over that.'

So we did. Bert went to his usual trouble of getting out the full tea service, properly brewed tea and rich tea biscuits. So I told him my story, right from the beginning. He listened attentively, interjecting every now and again a 'well I never'. After I'd finished we sat for a while in silence.

'They'd probably still give you the job.'

'The thing is Bert as far as any employer is concerned I am a murderer. My record says so.'

'Yes but everyone deserves a second chance.'

'Maybe I'll check it out. Nothing to lose after all.'

'That's the spirit.'

'Right I'll be off, and Bert, don't give up on the veg just yet.'

'Alright mate, just for you.'

That evening after the boys had gone to bed I sat down with Christine. I told her that much as I would like to stay I could not do so without an income. As I knew she would, she said it didn't matter about the money; that we would manage somehow. But I knew that she was barely managing at all before I came along and contributed to the household. She looked so miserable after this conversation, I told her what Bert had said about a job with the council. She seized on this straight away, although I explained they would never take on someone like me. She was more optimistic than me. Apparently several of the town councillors were members of Angela's congregation. Perhaps she could do something. She phoned her, and reported back that Angela was on the case, as she put it. The following evening just as we were settling down to watch television Angela appeared at the door. She had wasted no time:

'I've arranged an interview for you tomorrow with the town clerk and two of the councillors. Nine o'clock at the council offices.'

'Good grief. You don't waste any time. But do they know about me, my record?'

'I only spoke to one of the councillors who will be interviewing you. She was sympathetic. I think the feeling among a lot of people was that you were only charged this time because of your record. Once a murderer... You do realise that your previous conviction was mentioned in the paper after you were acquitted?'

'No I had no idea. I haven't seen a paper.'

'You can be sure the whole of the village knows all about you. So will you go for it?'

I agreed that I would. Christine was delighted. I was nervous. It turned out I needn't have been. The interview took place in an office in the town hall. It was clearly somewhere that was ordinarily used for another purpose. There was a line of grey filing cabinets along one wall and several stacks of boxes on the opposite one. The three of them sat behind a desk in front of the window. It was really too small for three people to sit behind and the set up looked incongruous. Apart from the town clerk, a man of about sixty, there was a male councillor, who looked like he wanted to be somewhere else, and a middle-aged woman who smiled sweetly at me throughout the interview. Neither of the councillors spoke. I sensed from the outset that there was a great deal of sympathy for me, and that the job was mine for the asking. I was asked a few questions, the answers to which they already knew, and told what the job entailed, which essentially was general labouring. So there it was, start Monday week. I couldn't wait to tell Christine but knowing I wouldn't see her until she came back from her job, I instead went to the vicarage.

'I expect you knew before I did, didn't you?'

'I knew they were well disposed to the idea of giving you a chance. I'm pleased for you Jim. A new beginning.'

'Thanks to you. You're a bit of a miracle worker. Before you know it, I'll be getting religion!'

'Maybe you will. Why don't you come to the church one Sunday? I know you like being in there. You could just sit at the back and see how it goes. You don't have to take part.'

'Perhaps I will. I owe you that much at least.'

24

It was nearly six months since I had last made the journey to London. Then it had been the dark of winter. Now it was the full heat of summer. The freshness of spring had gone but I still savoured the sights of the countryside; the burgeoning hedgerows, the ripened fields of wheat, the trees and woods, the glistening streams and rivers - 'each a glimpse and gone forever'. I hoped I would never grow tired of these bucolic delights, so long denied me. Inevitably I thought of Julia, and our little trips to the common. I had a lingering sense of guilt towards her. I felt as though I should have stayed and helped her in some way, although I don't know what I could have done. I felt I had deserted her; she who had been so kind to me. But I had just been released and my mind was both full of worries and empty of clear thoughts. In leaving prison I had carried on much as before. Never thinking too far into the future, acting on impulse. In this last year I had so often had the feeling that I wanted everything to just stop. Just stop to give me time to think, to see where I was headed, to make sensible decisions. I'm sure this sensation is shared by many people. As someone once said: 'life happens while you're busy making other plans'.

Part of my problem was my long imprisonment. I had thought about this a great deal, the effect it had on me, and no doubt others. I had concluded that you do not come out of prison a different person. You come out the same person in an older body. That's all. You do not grow and develop, through experience of life, like people outside. Your development stops the moment you are taken through the prison gates. Prison stunts your emotional growth. It must do. You have no opportunity to make your own decisions; decisions that will be tested by the vagaries and caprice of everyday life. So when I came out I was still twenty-five year old Jim. Perhaps that accounted for my immature thoughts and actions towards Alice.

Colette arrived home soon after me. She dropped her bags and threw her arms around me.

'So good to see you Jim.'

'Sorry about all the blabbing in court.'

She laughed, 'not the first time I've seen that, believe me. People like you are under an enormous amount of stress at times like that. It's a wonder there aren't more heart attacks in court.'

'Why? Are there any?'

'Oh yes, and strokes too. I worked really hard for one client, who was clearly not guilty, and who I was sure would be cleared but he had a stroke as he went into the witness box. Never regained consciousness.'

'How awful.'

'So you see, a few tears is nothing.'

'Anyway thanks again for all you've done.'

'Jim it was a pleasure. Christ, you deserve a break, for goodness sake. What happens now?'

'Well, I've got a job.'

'Great. Doing what?'

'Not sure really. It's working for the council in Saxmundham. Sweeping the streets probably. But the great thing is I'll be able to stay on there. I've grown really fond of the place, despite…'

Colette finished the sentence for me, 'despite being fitted up for murder.'

'When I get back I'm going to pay the police in Ipswich a visit, see what they're doing about Alice.'

'You might be wasting your time.'

'Why?'
'The case against her is entirely circumstantial. No forensic, no witnesses. The CPS won't stand for it, even if the police want to prosecute. Her defence would inevitably use the case against you to say that the real murderer got off.'
'I wonder how she can live with herself.'
'Perhaps one day she won't be able to.'
I stayed the night at Colette's. We slept together but there was no sex. We had formed a fondness for each other that somehow seemed to transcend the physical act. When I told Colette that I loved her I meant it in the full sense of the word. It was nothing to do with romantic love, or lust, but to do with how you regarded the other person. It was in a sense a developed form of liking, born out of respect for the kind of person the other was; a respect for their kindness, their warmth and generosity, their ability to give without thought of reward, and such a person was Colette. We talked long into the night. I wondered how long she would go on working.
'Do you think you'll ever retire?'
'Never thought about it but if I did what would I do? Answer: end up down in the country being bored out of my mind.'
'Do you and Geoffrey get on? I mean, are you still intimate?'
She laughed. 'What a funny way you have of putting things, Jim. Yes, every now and again but I don't think Geoffrey's too bothered. It sometimes seems like a duty he's doing. I wonder if he isn't a repressed homosexual.'
'Why do you say that?'
'You have to understand that nearly his whole life has been spent in male company; prep school, public school, the army. Plenty of opportunity there to form strong bonds. When his army pals come to stay there's a sort of intimacy between them all that there never is between Geoffrey and me.'
'Does it bother you?'
'No, not really. He's a very decent man. He's never once been violent towards me or barely ever raised his voice. He lets me

do whatever I want, come and go as I please, have sex with people I meet on a train.'

That made me laugh. 'So does he know about me?'

'No, and he wouldn't be interested. If he did know he wouldn't be bothered.'

'Sounds like you're well matched. What about children? Did neither of you want to have any?'

'You know it's funny, the subject never came up. I suppose that means we weren't that interested in propagating ourselves.'

'You don't regret it now?'

'Not in the least. I think my maternal gene might be absent.'

'Well your loving gene isn't.'

When I left the next morning I held her close and told her that I hoped we would remain friends for the rest of our lives. Her response was that she was in no doubt that it would be so, and made me promise to come and see her often.

In Ipswich I went to the office in Friars Street. It was closed. I went round to Tacket Street. Judith and Ann seemed pleased to see me. I asked about Friars Street. Apparently Alice had gone there immediately after the trial, sacked Siobhan and closed the office.

'What about you two? Is she intending to keep this one on?'

'We think so. She said something about moving the stuff over from Friars Street. The computer's here already. She got that moved after you were arrested.'

'So you're managing OK?'

'Why Jim, are you thinking of asking for your old job back?'

This raised a laugh. 'No, but I tell you what, I never got paid a penny. Do you think I should pop round to see her and demand my wages?' More laughter. I was hoping to see Siobhan and thank her for her testimony. Have you got her phone number?'

They had and gave it to me. 'We would have gladly testified for you Jim but obviously Siobhan knew you better than us. We thought the whole trial was a farce. What we want to know is what the police are going to do about her.'

'That's what I'd like to know. In fact I'm going to the police station now to ask them just that. I'll let you know what they say.'

Ipswich police station was one of those 1960s buildings of glass and metal which even when it was new had an insubstantial look about it. By the time of my visit the fragility of its construction was beginning to show with peeling paint and spalling brickwork giving an air of dilapidation. At the front desk I asked for Inspector Lambert. It was clear that I was recognised and there followed a *sotto voce* conversation between the constable and the sergeant on duty. A phone call was made, equally low volume, after which I was told that the inspector was not available. An older man, who also recognised me, came into the office. Another conversation took place between this man and the sergeant, after which the older man came over, introduced himself as Superintendent Fellowes, and suggested that we went to his office. I thought that a man of his rank might have been entitled to a somewhat larger space than the office into which he led me. There was just room for a desk, three chairs and a couple of filing cabinets. There was paper everywhere, on every surface, and even piles on the floor.

I couldn't help but ask: 'how do you keep track of everything?'

He laughed, 'with difficulty. You wouldn't believe the amount of paper a case generates these days, especially anything financial. Anyway, you haven't come here to talk about my paperwork. What can I do for you?'

'I think you know what I'm going to say but I'll say it anyway. What are you going to do about Alice, Mrs Dalby?'

He sighed, took off his glasses and rubbed his hand over his face. 'The answer is nothing. The CPS wouldn't stand another trial. Lambert still thinks you did it, by the way, but I don't. To tell you the truth, I rather took my eye off the ball while the investigation was going on. My time was taken up with a very complicated fraud case involving millions. By the time I got round to looking at things the CPS had given the go ahead. I'm surprised they did. It was never a substantial case. Too much credence was given to Mrs Dalby's evidence.'

'So she's going to get away with murder, even though everybody now knows she did it?'

'Knowing something is not the same as evidence. There is even less evidence against her than there was against you. In your case there was at least some forensic. All the evidence against her is circumstantial. If we did prosecute, a major theme, in fact the major theme of the defence would be your trial. If the prosecution were so convinced that Mrs Dalby murdered her husband, why prosecute Mallinson? That's what they would ask.'

'No doubt part of the reason for going ahead with the prosecution was the fact that I'm a convicted murderer.'

'No doubt it was.'

'Well here's something to chew on. Not only am I not a murderer, but the murder for which I was convicted was also carried out by Alice.'

Once I had established that he had sufficient time, I told him the long, sorry tale. He was clearly fascinated.

'So there you are superintendent, I bet you've never heard a story like that in all your long career.'

I was not entirely surprised by the unwillingness of the police to investigate further but it did seem a monstrance injustice that Dalby's death should go unpunished. I dare say that had Dalby had more in the way of relatives more of a fuss might have been made. In fact his parents were long dead and he had just one sister, who lived in Australia. As for myself, thoughts of revenge for this further wrong that had been done to me at Alice's hands, were nowhere to be found. I felt as though I was on the verge of something, a point of change in my life which would give me the solace that I had craved since first entering prison. I now had this job, such as it was, and there was Christine, a person so completely good that I was fearful that my own inadequacies would disqualify me from ever having the kind of relationship with her that I hoped might be possible. With this prospect in view, the thought of inflicting some kind of rough justice on Alice was of no interest to me.

On my first day in my new job I was introduced to the other members of the team, if a total of three persons can be considered a team. There was Bev, who it seems, was the boss, Dennis and me. We were based at the Market Hall, which, as I was told, was the cultural and community centre of the village. According to Bev my duties were doing anything she asked me to do. She said this in a light hearted way which made me laugh and I thought to myself that we would get on well. More specifically there was maintenance and cleaning of the hall, litter picking in the town centre and attention to the various flower beds around the village. I spent my first day cleaning the hall with the other two following the function that had been held there on the Saturday. I quickly learnt by the way they went about their work that the other two were proud of their village and expected me to be the same. There was no idle slacking or resentment of the boss, whoever that was, but an easy contentment in doing a job well. Bev, I suppose was about forty-five, thickening round the middle as so many middle aged women do, but with a young face framed by dark curls. Dennis, who I seldom saw without a roll-up in his hand or mouth, was a long, gangling type of fellow, about the same age as Bev. I had been working with them for more than two weeks before I realised they were husband and wife. Ever after I could only think of them as Jack Spratt and his wife, and in fact on one occasion I did call Dennis Jack. He didn't seem to notice.
As the days went by I grew to love the job. Bev and Dennis, once they realised that I would work as enthusiastically as them, were friendly and helpful. But what I liked about the job was the number of people I met during the course of the day, especially when I was working outside. I was in a sense a celebrity. Pretty well everyone in the village knew who I was and I had the feeling that the majority were well disposed to me. Very few people would pass without a greeting and I soon got to know

people by sight. The shopkeepers were always friendly. They appreciated the street outside their premises being clean and litter free. I could never have imagined that such a menial job could bring such rewards but I guess it was mostly in the way I regarded the work and what it meant to me by way of being able to stay at Christine's. Our relationship was much as it had been before I went to Chelmsford. We had settled into a routine that was comfortable for both of us. I got on well with the boys when our paths crossed but it seemed they were little interested in forming some kind of deeper relationship with me. They were remarkably autonomous, having had to become so following the death of their father. And so the days passed and it must have been three or four weeks after I had started my job that I remembered Angela's invitation to come to a service one Sunday.

I sat at the back of the church and didn't participate in the kneeling and standing nor in the singing. It was just pleasant to be in that space again and feel the music and singing waft over me. Once the congregation had departed Angela came to join me. We kissed, she sat down beside me and began with, 'well?'
'I enjoyed the sermon. You're really putting the boot into the rich, aren't you?'
'Well you know what it says in the bible.'
'You mean the eye of the needle and all that. Yes, well not much notice of that taken of that these days. Do you just trot that sermon out when you need a bit more in the collection plate?'
'Very funny. Unfortunately it doesn't work.'
'Tell me something, how many of your congregation do you think actually believe all that stuff, about heaven and hell and God?'
'Never thought about that before. I would think the majority believe.'
'And what about you?'
There was a very long pause while Angela stared at me before speaking.

'If you repeat any of this I will personally come and strangle you. The answer is that no, I don't believe in a God, heaven, life after death, or anything metaphysical. In fact I fail to understand how any intelligent person does believe in those things. There that's shocked you, hasn't it?'

'Actually it hasn't. So thinking about the clergy in general, how many do you imagine think like you.'

Once again a long pause. 'Making a bit of a wild guess, I would say a third are like me, a third believe, and the remainder try not to think about it.'

'In view of your non-belief why do you carry on?'

'You can imagine I've asked myself that question plenty of times. The church is a comfort to a lot of people, especially to the lonely and bereaved. It's also a focus for the community. We have different groups meeting here. All in all I think what I do is worthwhile, faith or not. Anyway, time to ask you a question. How are you getting on with Christine?'

'Fine.'

She seemed to be waiting for something more. 'What?'

'Just fine?'

'She's lovely, we get on very well. What are you getting at?'

'She loves you, Jim. When are you going to make a move?'

There was a silence while I tried to marshal my thoughts. I didn't know quite how to put things and before I could spit out the words Angela spoke again.

'Do you want a relationship with Christine or not?'

'I want that more than anything. I haven't met such a kind, warm, generous person during the whole of my life but I'm scared.'

'Of what?'

'Look at my life, what a mess I've made of it. Fourteen years gone down a black hole, and the rest getting mixed up twice with a homicidal maniac. I'm forty years of age and what have I achieved so far – a job sweeping the streets.'

'I thought you liked the job.'

'I do, I love it, but it's not much to offer someone. Is it?'

'You idiot. Do you understand what love is? It's about loving someone, not despite their faults, but because of them. Love doesn't have reservations.'
'I'm terrified that I will make a mess of things again and end up hurting someone that, to use your word, I love.'
'So you love Christine too.'
'Of course I do. How could I not?'
'So what's stopping you?'
I had no answer.
'Jim, speak to her soon.'
The subject of speaking to Christine occupied my thoughts for the next few days. On the Wednesday I bought a bottle of wine, and once we had settled down to watch television I brought it out.
'Special occasion Jim? What are we celebrating?'
We often had a few glasses of wine at the weekend but never during the week. I didn't answer but poured us both a glass. Mine was gone in seconds and I poured myself another.
'What's up? Are you trying to get drunk?'
'Dutch courage.'
'What do you need Dutch courage for?'
And then I blurted it out, 'Christine I love you. Please forgive me for rejecting you that other time. I want more than anything to be with you. Will you forgive me?'
'Oh Jim, nothing to forgive.'
We kissed and cuddled and giggled our way thought the rest of the evening. I could sense the relief in Christine was equal to my own. I kept cautioning myself. Don't do or say anything stupid. Don't spoil this. We didn't make love for the first time until a few days later. When it happened it was as wonderful as I imagined it would be. In the following days I felt happier than I thought it possible to be. It seemed at last that I had found what I somehow instinctively and perhaps unconsciously had been seeking along. I felt profoundly contented.

<h1 style="text-align:center">25</h1>

I would occasionally see Alice as I went about the town, but always from a distance, until one day in the supermarket trying to choose a bottle of wine I found a small person standing next to me. It was Rosie. Before I had the chance to say anything to her, Alice and Tess came round the end of the aisle. I didn't want to hang around but as I left I couldn't help noticing a change in Alice. She looked a lot thinner and had a downturn in the corners of her mouth that I had never noticed before and worry lines round her eyes. It was probably another year before I bumped into her again, this time face to face, as she came out of the supermarket wheeling a trolley. We stopped facing each other. She looked awful, even thinner than before and looking ten years older. She spoke first.

'Hello Jim. How have you been?'

'I'm alright but what about you?'

'I'm a fright aren't I?'

'What's happened?'

She ignored my question. 'Will you give me a hand to put these things in my car?'

I went to take the trolley from her.

'No, I need the trolley to lean on. Just come with me and put the things in the boot, if you will.'

I did as she said.

'Have you got a minute? I don't often get the chance to talk to someone. There's a bench over there. We could sit for a minute.'
I didn't know how to refuse. We walked across to the bench, she leaning heavily on my arm. Before she sat she took out a small cushion and put it on the bench.
'I need this now. Got no flesh left on my arse.'
'What's happened? What's wrong with you?'
'No-one knows. Been to every doctor, specialist you can think of. Had any number of tests, x-rays, scans, the lot. Can't find anything wrong with me. I expect it's my punishment for leading such an evil life. What do you think? I expect you think I deserve this.'
I chose not to answer. 'Where are the girls?'
'They're with my brother. I think they will be there for good now.'
'I thought you didn't get on with him.'
'It's not him really. It's his wife. Anyway they love the girls, and they love being with their two.'
'So, on your own now.'
She sighed. 'You're sitting next to an idiot who has destroyed her own life as well as two others. But you're alright now aren't you?'
'Yes, but no thanks to you.'
'I don't expect you to believe this, but I'm really pleased for you. Anyway by bum's starting to complain.'
I helped her get up. She seemed incapable of doing so on her own.
'I usually have a stick with me. Jim would you come and see me some time? I get so terribly lonely now.'
'Alice shouldn't you be in some kind of nursing home, where you can be looked after properly?'
'Probably. I expect I'm in denial that I'm dying, and probably soon. But will you come and see me, maybe next Friday?'
The correct, the only answer was of course no, a resounding no, but she looked so pathetic, so defeated I couldn't say it, so I settled for a 'maybe'. I saw her to her car, where before getting

in she kissed me on the lips. I watched her drive away, my head full of thoughts and memories. It had been an upsetting experience, which Christine immediately sensed when I got home. Christine was not a person to get angry or even raise her voice, but when I told her what I'd agreed to, she called me a bloody fool and stormed off upstairs. The coolness between us lasted a day or so, but then reasserted itself as Friday approached. Was I being a bloody fool?

The door to No.17 was ajar. My knock was answered by a call to come in. Alice was in the living room, lying on the sofa, totally naked.

'Don't worry Jim. I'm not trying to seduce you. I just wanted you to see the reality of what I have become.'

And what she had become made a shocking sight. Her ribs were pushing through a skin that was almost transparent. Her breasts had shrivelled to practically nothing. Her stomach was concave and her arms and legs were no more than sticks. Perhaps most shocking of all was the fact that she was almost completely bald, a fact disguised on our last meeting by the wig sitting on the sofa beside her. She slowly raised herself up, put on the wig before anything else, and then her nightdress and dressing gown.

'That's the worst indignity for a woman, losing her hair. Would you like a drink?'

Before I could answer she poured two glasses. I could see that it was one of Dalby's special wines, from the Médoc.

'No weedkiller in it then?'

'If there is, I'll be drinking it too.'

'Maybe you want to kill yourself and take me with you.'

'No Jim. I've got things to sort out before I go. Come on, have a drink with me.'

I did so and we sat in silence for a while.

'Will you come and sit with me Jim?'

I went across to the sofa.

'Hold me, please. I just want to feel the touch of another person.'

I put my arms around her. She was all angles and sharpness and I noticed for the first time a smell. It wasn't the smell of a dirty body but rather the odour of decay. Her body was rotting from within. We sat for a while and then I noticed that she had fallen asleep. She awoke after about half an hour and apologised. We separated and she poured more wine.

'Weedkiller starting to take effect yet?'

It was a poor attempt at a joke.

'Why did you do it Alice? Why kill Adrian? He loved you. He adored the girls. He would have given you anything, done anything for you.'

'Who can explain the workings of the mind of a madwoman? It seemed logical at the time. I think I must be a psychopath. I had grown tired of him. He was everything you say but I needed something more, some sort of challenge. I told you that we stopped having sex because I was depressed but it was more than that. In the end I couldn't bear him touching me. It was like an overeager dog wanting to please. The more he tried to please me the more repulsive I found him. In the end we just stopped altogether. And he was so boring. Those stories that he told, that even you heard several times. Imagine how many more times I had heard them.'

'He was a good man, simple but good, and you destroyed him for nothing.'

'Yes all true, and I tried to destroy you too. Like I said, I think there's something wrong with me.'

I got up to go.

'Jim will you come again. It's been so nice this little moment together. Will you, please?'

She suggested the following Friday. I said I would think about it but I knew I would go. How could I explain this to Christine? I couldn't of course. It made me seem as crazy as Alice clearly was. This time the coolness lasted the whole week. Nothing was said except on the Friday, just as I was leaving, 'Jim, it's a trap.' But it wasn't, at least not then. I made a resolve that this would be the last time, whatever ensued. As I approached the house once more I noticed a car parked in the street outside. Once again the door was ajar and my knock was answered by a smartly dressed man. It seemed that he was just leaving.

'Is everything clear then, Mr Radcliffe?'

Mr Radcliffe confirmed that it was.

'My solicitor,' Alice explained, 'getting everything sorted out before the inevitable

This time she was dressed in one of her pretty summer frocks but it hung about her in formless folds. There was a bottle and two glasses on the little table before the sofa.

'This is the last of Adrian's special bottles. Will you share it with me?'

She poured without waiting for an answer and tapped the sofa beside her.

'Please, will you?'

We sat and drank without speaking and after a while she leaned against me and fell asleep once more. When she woke the wig had slipped sideways on her head, and this together with her skull-like face gave her a comically grotesque appearance, as though from a horror film.

'On Monday I'm going into a hospice in Ipswich. They're sending a car to collect me and my few bits.'

'What about the house?'

'Radcliffe is going to sell it, and all the contents.'

'I suppose everything will go to the girls.'

'Mostly, yes. What am I going to tell them?'

'About what?'

'About me and my life.'

'I don't think you're asking the right person.'

'Who else can I ask? I haven't got a friend in the world. We never really made friends here in Saxmundham and since the trial… well you can imagine.'

'What do they know about Adrian?'

'Just that he fell ill and died. But what can I tell them about me, what I've done?'

'Maybe tell them nothing. If they are curious they may start asking questions in later life but for now, least said the better, I would think.'

I got up to go. She clung to my arm.

'Jim, I'm frightened.'

Despite myself, I couldn't help feeling sorry for this wreck of a person but there was nothing more to be said or done here. I eased myself away from her. She followed me to the front door.

'Goodbye Alice.'

'Yes, this really is goodbye Jim, isn't it?'

Walking down the path I turned to see her standing there looking after me. I walked slowly into town, unable to get out of my mind that last grotesque image of her standing by the doorway with the lopsided wig on her ravaged face.

Less than a month later I received a message from her brother. Alice's funeral was to be at Ipswich crematorium the following week. It was inevitable that I would go. The crematorium was on the outskirts of the town, not far from Westerfield station, so I decided to take a train there and walk. I never tired of being out in the open, whatever the weather. On this day there was a pale sun shining through a cirrus sky and a freshening breeze stirring the leaves, and as I walked I recalled once more the events that had brought me to this point. How could I have ever imagined that meeting Laura at that party all those years ago could have caused all that had followed? And now finally here I was at the funeral of my nemesis.

There was less than a dozen people outside the chapel when I arrived. I recognised no-one except Judith and Ann from the Ipswich office. I went over to them. Ann spoke before I could, 'Surprised to see us here, Jim?'

'Well…'

'She turned up trumps in the end. When she sold the business she insisted that the new owner keep us on. And she gave us each a thousand pound bonus. So turning up today, least we could do. But then what are you doing here?'

'I know it's odd isn't it, after everything. I saw her a couple of times recently. She was in a terrible state. Full of contrition but of course far too late. In the end she was the victim.'

We moved inside. The service was very short and afterwards everyone dispersed. Clearly there was to be no wake. A couple who I had assumed to be Alice's brother and partner moved in my direction. The man held out his hand: 'Kevin, Alice's brother. It's Jim isn't it?'

I confirmed that it was.

'How are you now?'

'I'm very well. Everything's good, thanks.'

'I'm pleased about that. The damage that she wrought…You know, she was the same as a child, sly and devious. We never got on. And now it's all ended. You know she believed that the wasting disease was her punishment. I think it was all in her head. The guilt was too difficult to bear. It destroyed her.'

'It would seem that way. How are the girls?'

'They're OK. We didn't want to bring them today. It would have been too upsetting. We just hope they'll adjust to us being their parents from now on. Thankfully they're great friends with Julian and Sarah, which has been a big help.'

'Well, say hello from Uncle Jim.'

We parted and I walked back to the station. I had a tremendous feeling of lightness. I felt as though I had been in a battle that I had won against all the odds. But then later as the train rattled back through the countryside the lightness disappeared, to be replaced by a sense of sadness so strong that it quite overpowered me and I started to weep, and two words echoed round inside my head – waste and loss, waste and loss.

26

About a year after Alice's funeral I heard from Radcliffe. He asked me to go to his office where he told me that Alice had left me a substantial sum in her will. He thought it would amount to about a quarter of a million pounds, once probate had finally been sorted out. He also gave me an envelope which contained a document written by Alice, signed by her and witnessed by him. In this document she confessed to having committed both murders. Radcliffe told me that a second copy had been sent to the senior police officer at Ipswich. Some months later I received the money, which indeed amounted to a quarter of a million pounds, slightly more in fact. Christine and I had decided that all the money would go to charities which help ex-prisoners.

After Angela was ordained in 1994 we insisted that Christine and I be the first couple she married. In 1996 she herself was married, to her girlfriend Melanie. In 1995 Briony realised her ambition to become a barrister and Jessica joined the civil service. In 2002 Dave died of a heart attack. He had never stopped drinking. In the same year the Town Clerk's post at Saxmundham became vacant. I applied and much to everyone's surprise was given the job. In 2003 James qualified as a civil engineer and went off to work in Norwich. Harry graduated two years later and moved to London to work in finance. About this time I heard from Colette that she had retired and given up the flat in London. I retired in 2011 and Christine in 2016. We spent all our free time exploring the countryside of Suffolk and Norfolk. Nature and wildlife had become our passion. We were extremely happy.

But then, about two years ago, the dreams started. Always the same. Alice comes to me, the old, voluptuous Alice. She wants to make love for one last time. She gets into bed with me. Our love making is just as it used to be but when I open my eyes I see that she is just a skeleton, my fingers interlaced with the bones of her ribcage, her grinning skull pressed against my face. I try to scream but nothing comes out until I wake up sweating and panicking. It is the same every night. Christine is no longer able to sleep in the same bed with me. I dread going to sleep. I stay up watching television and drinking. It's affecting my health. I'm losing weight. Too thin the doctor says. He gives me useless pills. I see no way forward.

Is this it then? Is this the trap?

<u>Acknowledgement</u>

This is my first novel and throughout the writing of it I was supported and encouraged by Chris, my wife. She also proof read the draft twice, pointing out my many errors and making suggestions for improvements. My heartfelt thanks go to her.